Found Things

Found Things

Marilyn Hilton

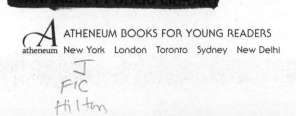

ATHENEUM BOOKS FOR YOUNG READERS
atheneum New York London Toronto Sydney New Delhi

For Ann and Steven, who were my first best friends

ATHENEUM BOOKS FOR YOUNG READERS
An imprint of Simon & Schuster Children's Publishing Division
1230 Avenue of the Americas, New York, New York 10020

For information about special discounts for bulk purchases, please
contact Simon & Schuster Special Sales at 1-866-506-1949 or
business@simonandschuster.com.
The Simon & Schuster Speakers Bureau can bring authors to your live
event. For more information or to book an event, contact the
Simon & Schuster Speakers Bureau at 1-866-248-3049 or visit our
website at www.simonspeakers.com.
Book design by Debra Sfetsios-Conover
The text for this book is set in Cochin LT Std.
Manufactured in the United States of America
0814 FFG

10 9 8 7 6 5 4 3 2
Library of Congress Cataloging-in-Publication Data
Hilton, Marilyn.
Found things / Marilyn Hilton.
p. cm.
Summary: Eleven-year-old River Rose, bullied at school and missing
her older brother, Theron, makes friends with a strange new classmate,
Meadow Lark, and the two search for a miracle by floating wishes down
the river.
ISBN 978-1-4424-6087-4 (hardcover)
ISBN 978-1-4424-6089-8 (eBook)
[1. Best friends—Fiction. 2. Friendship—Fiction. 3. Family life—New
Hampshire—Fiction. 4. Wishes—Fiction. 5. Brothers and sisters—
Fiction. 6. Identity—Fiction. 7. New Hampshire—Fiction.] I. Title.
PZ7.H56774Fou   2014
[Fic]—dc23
2013019360

"Hope" is the thing with feathers-
That perches in the soul-

— Emily Dickinson

Chapter 1

The morning after Theron leave us, I start talking this way — like no one else I'd ever known in Quincely, New Hampshire. Whenever Mama heard me, she look like she just ate a purple plum and didn't know what to do with the memory of it, all sweet and sour mixed together in her mouth. But the only thing she say was that miracles are what's left after everything else is used up, and one morning I'd wake up and talk just like her River again.

I noticed that she never say one day a miracle would bring Theron back to us. Maybe that was too much to hope for. Theron leave us in early March, and the hole that remain grew wider and deeper and more raggedy as each day pass.

By mid-May he still hadn't returned, but I found out there were worse things than talking peculiar. I could have been that new girl, Meadow Lark, with the popped-out eye and her lurchy way of walking.

She have a pretty name but it was one of the only things pretty about her. In homeroom she stood up and introduce herself, just like everyone had to do on their first day. Meadow Lark Frankenfield smiled when she say her name, not like most new kids, who stoop and mumble, or look at their shoes and turn red, and then collapse into their seats and cross their arms. Meadow Lark kept standing, and touch her blue-frame glasses as if she expected questions. But no one ask her anything.

Most kids probably couldn't have told you her real name thirty seconds later, but by F period, just before lunch, they were already calling her Frankenfemme. Daniel Bunch started that. He say it was a French word. I don't know French, but you could tell he'd already drawn out a space and put Meadow Lark where she belong in it.

Anytime a new kid start, everyone who is already here rubs the smudges off themselves and act like the spoons from the good drawer, a little shinier than the everyday ones. Sonya Mittell bounces her pony-tail higher, DeWayne Green puts more drama into his jokes, and Martin Delboni hunches deeper into his shoulders. Teachers talk like radio ads and show more gum when they smile and call on everybody, not just the usual kids. Everyone brightens up when a new kid start, because they want the new kid to go home and say what a great school it is and what interesting and shiny people go there.

But for Meadow Lark Frankenfield, that didn't happen. If it didn't happen the first day, it wouldn't ever happen. Something was wrong with her—not just her popped-out eye, but with her whole body. She walked as if her leg was glued on backward, like a car rolling along with a flat tire.

I was eating lunch in the quad and watching her that first day, when Daniel Bunch come by.

"I see you looking at Frankenfemme," he say, sounding so proud of the name he'd given her. No one but Daniel ever talked to me at lunch anymore, though you could never call what we say much of a conversation. "Taking notes?"

I had just bitten into my sandwich when he come along. I looked down at my sneakers and chewed, wishing he'd just go away. I didn't want to see him, and I didn't want to see that cast on his arm because it reminded me too much of Theron.

But he stopped in front of me, and I felt his stare. "You two have a lot in common, she being the same kind of trash as you."

Then he got up real close to my face and whispered, "You know what your brother is, right?"

Keep looking down, River, I told myself, as the sandwich in my hand quivered. I thought of all the things Daniel might call Theron—a runaway, a coward, a fugitive—or maybe he was about to call him trash, too. I'd heard all of them, but I wouldn't have called my brother any of them.

"I'll tell you," Daniel say. "A wimp."

He is not a wimp, I thought, and blinked.

Daniel tapped his cast. "And a drunk—the worst kind of drunk, the kind that drives into rivers and then runs away. If he ever comes back here, he'll pay for it. They'll throw him in jail for it."

Daniel kept his face up to mine, like he was waiting for me to say something, and hoping I'd look at him. All I could think about at that moment was not inhaling his ham-and-mustard-smelling breath and not crying in front of him. And that he could have come up with a better word than "wimp." Funny that Daniel thought he was so smart, when everybody knew he had to repeat fourth grade.

"And don't clamp your jaw like that," he told me.

My eyes squeezed narrow, and I pressed my sandwich until the jelly oozed out. Theron started paying for what he did the night it happened, and none of those words—"runaway," "deserter," "fugitive," "wimp," or "drunk"—were true. They couldn't be.

Theron. The thought of him caught my heart.

Finally, after what felt longer than January, Daniel pulled away, but he left his nasty breath with me.

So when Meadow Lark come over and sit beside me on the bench a few minutes later and held out her open bag of Cheetos, I got up and went to Ms. Zucchero's room to work on my collage.

No one else was there except Ms. Zucchero, who ate carrots one by one from a lunch bag while grading artwork, so I sat at the big butcher-block table in the middle and spread out my collage. I'd put almost everything I'd ever found on that collage. It was going to be a present to Mama, so it had to be perfect and it had to make her smile.

I laid the little string of gold-colored beads, the bent watch face, and the tiny key on the table. I took six colored pens from the bin and set them down. Glue, scissors, colored paper, paper punches next to them, and then I started to sort, and place and replace, and then glue and write.

Lately when I worked like that, something strange happened. It was hard to understand, but my mind wandered around inside a house. I'd never seen that house before, but it felt as familiar as the smell of my pillow. My mind slipped into that house and walked around in it while my hands worked, so stealthily that I never realized I was there until something interrupted me.

That day while I worked on my collage, my mind went to a pantry room off the kitchen. This was a new room, but I could tell you everything in that pantry (cans of Campbell's soup and Ever Fresh tomatoes, blue-and-white sacks of flour and pink sacks of sugar, and store-brand Cheerios and oatmeal), the color of the walls (spring-leaf green), and the smell when you go near the shelves (onions and oregano).

Ms. Zucchero say something to me, and quick as spit I was back in the art room and realized I'd been in the pantry of that house.

"Tell me about the beads." Ms. Zucchero was pointing to the three gold-colored beads on a string. Her fingernails were painted dark purple, and the one she pointed with had a little chip.

The glue the beads sat in was still white, and I pressed them until they hurt my finger.

"I found them in the river. They're just plastic."

She leaned over the beads for a few seconds. "No, I think these beads are real gold. My aunt had some just like them. What else did you find?"

I looked at everything glued onto my collage, and pointed out each one to her one by one. The glass pieces—green, red, purple, deep blue—all brushed soft by the water and sand of the river. The porcelain doll head with the nose buffed off, the piece of wood that looked like a hand, the tiny bald plastic baby with arms and legs and head that moved, a black bear's tooth, the peach-colored leaf that was still soft, an *R* typewriter key, a bottle stopper made of glass, the bent watch face, the stone that looked like a face, the gold-colored beads.

Ms. Zucchero put her hands behind her back and took another close look. "They all tell a story, don't they?" she say, and then went back to her desk.

"I guess so." I never thought they had a story. They just showed up on the sandy beach at the river.

"I hope I can hear that story one day."

The wall clock say it was almost time for A period, but I wanted to glue one more thing, a tiny metal iron, before then. And I wanted to go back to that pantry, where behind the flour was a jar of chocolate bits that I knew tasted bittersweet. Instead I thought about Meadow Lark Frankenfield and how I'd left her on the bench by herself—but not before I smiled just enough to let her know I knew what she did for me.

Meadow Lark wasn't pretty, but you could tell she was a cared-about girl by the straight cut of her pumpkin-colored hair and her smooth fingernails. And that bag of Cheetos come out of a paper bag with her name written in curlicues. When she pulled out the Cheetos, a napkin fell out with a tiny red heart drawn in the corner. Someone cared about Meadow Lark and whether she had nice hair and fingernails and a good snack. But even though she come over to the bench after Daniel went away, I knew that her eye and the crooked way she walked would take some getting used to.

Chapter 2

"Daddy," I asked that night, "am I pretty?"

"Everything about you is pretty, River," he say. "Especially your name."

Daddy told me all the time how when he and Mama brought me home that first day after they knew I was theirs, they didn't change my name because it was already too perfect. I knew that like I knew the sound of their voices, but that night I needed to hear it again.

Then, as always, Daddy and I got quiet and listened to the dusk. That's when the things of the day and the things of the night switch places, and everything blurs. It's when Daddy rolls back the awning over the deck and we watch the stars grow in the sky. It's the time of day, Mama say, when angels abound, and if you're very still you can hear the rustle of their wings descending.

Sometimes I wondered what Daddy thought

about at dusk, now that Theron was gone. Did he think about Theron and where he might be, and how Daddy didn't stop Theron when he say he was leaving us and promised he'd never come back? That's what I thought about, but I knew dusk was a special time for Daddy—almost a sacred time—so I never asked him about those things on my mind.

After night settled over the sky and tucked us under it, when it was okay to talk again, I asked Daddy if he'd ever seen an angel.

His mouth wrestled a smile. "Besides the one I'm looking at now?"

When he talked like that, I knew that I, too, was a cared-about girl, even with that feeling in the back of my heart that I belonged somewhere else.

Then he leaned over so far to me that his beach chair squeaked and say very low, "Between you and me, I don't believe in them."

At that, Mama's voice come through the kitchen window behind us. "Ingram, you can't find what you're not looking for," she say as one plate clacked against another. "But if you look hard enough, you'll find it."

Mama was always saying things like that—don't wash your hair every day, be kind to your enemies, forgive and be free—and now this: You can't find it if you're not looking for it.

Daddy shrugged and then whispered, "She believes, and that's all that matters."

I looked up at the sky, which was mute and dotted with stars. I wanted to believe like Mama did in invisible things, and I wanted to believe that Theron might one day come back to us. So, even though I had as much confidence as Daddy in angels and miracles, I found a star and whispered so soft that anyone listening would have had to read my lips, "I wish I had the eyes to see."

When I walked past Theron's room on my way to bed, his smell was, as usual, still there. Cinnamon toothpaste, sweaty sneakers, and his shampoo with the pine-tree fragrance. And that sun-warm-skin smell that's only his. Theron's scents hovering in his room made me ache to see him again. I stepped one foot inside and touched the things on his bureau that he touched probably every day: his hairbrush, his silver dollar from the river, his picture of Shawna, the all-star trophy he got after he began to "straighten up," as Daddy call it.

I stretched my arm to touch the spot on his trophy he'd have touched so many times — on the shoulder of the baseball player winding up for a pitch. It would be just like Theron to touch the shoulder. Other people might have remembered different things about Theron, and some of them not very nice, but what I remembered was his hand on someone's shoulder.

"River Rose Byrne, don't you put another finger on that statue!"

How Mama slipped up the stairs so softly was one of the great mysteries of the ages. She stood in the hall with her hands on her hips, the silhouette of her head blocking out the ceiling light.

My hand snapped back. "I just—"

"I know what you're up to. You keep your hands off your brother's things. What will he do when he comes back and sees fingerprint smudges on his trophy?"

"Probably turn around and go back to where he come from."

I expected Mama to say, "*Came*, River," as usual, but instead she dropped her hands from her hips and pressed her lips together tight, and I realized that was exactly what Mama feared. I wanted to say, *Mama, don't get your hopes up so, because I don't believe he'll ever come home. He left here so mad and determined, so full of pepper and pain, that we will never see him again.*

Instead I say, "I was only kidding, Mama," because what else could I tell her as she stood in Theron's doorway with her face so full of wishing for him to come home?

Chapter 3

I couldn't stop thinking about what Mama and Daddy say about angels and being watchful. As if my wish began to draw breath while I slept, the next day I decided to focus my eyes in a new way. The first thing I noticed when I woke up was that Mama wasn't humming in the kitchen. For as long as I could remember, every morning Mama had hummed in the kitchen, but this morning I realized that she hadn't done that since Theron went away. Most times I didn't want to hear it anyway, being so sleepy that it made my bones itch, but this morning I realized how much I missed that sound.

Mama wasn't even in the kitchen that morning. I found her sitting on her bed, tracing her finger along the chenille pattern of their bedspread. The room smelled spicy of aftershave, and Daddy come out of their bathroom smoothing the gray hair above his ear.

"Where you going today?" I asked.

"Just down the track to Boston."

We both looked at Mama, and I say to her, "Don't worry—he'll be back tonight."

Daddy worked as a train porter, and Boston was one of his shortest runs. When he went down to Boston, he was back home again almost before we knew he had gone. It was like he had a regular job.

"I know that," Mama say, and nodded. "Just please, Ingram, don't be late coming home."

There was a look between them then, as alive as a violin string pulling out a last note, that made me hold my breath until Daddy answered her. "As long as there's coal in the bin and the rails don't buckle." It was what he always say when she worried that he wouldn't come back.

Mama smiled, and my new eyes opened again and saw that she was wearing her red lipstick. She looked so pretty. Maybe she wanted Daddy to think so too, so that when he traveled far away, he'd always want to come home.

At school I watched the clumps of kids in the quad before the first bell, and the teachers in my classes, and then my tennis shoes running the track in PE. I imagined looking at everyone through the prism

Mama kept on the kitchen windowsill, all of them appearing stretched and rainbow. Seeing things differently wasn't so hard. The hard part was knowing exactly what I was looking for, though I sensed it could be right around the corner.

That good feeling lasted only until lunch, when Daniel come to me again and my day shrank into its usual colors. I rubbed my apple hard on my sleeve, to make it look like I didn't notice him, but that didn't work. As he strolled by me, he muttered, "I'm watching you. Always watching you," spending extra time on each *W* sound.

After he passed, I looked up and saw Meadow Lark Frankenfield. Just like the day before, she come and sat on my bench and opened her curlicue bag.

I wanted Cheetos today and would have taken one when she offered it, but instead she pulled out a bag of pretzel sticks. Pretzel sticks are what you get when everything else in the snack pack is gone. So when she pulled open the bag of pretzels and held it out to me, I stared at her. I stared and didn't say a word. It felt good.

Then she looked away and reached into that bag and put a pretzel stick in her mouth. As she did, a strand of her hair slipped in with it. It had felt good to stare and not say a word when she held out that sad bag of pretzel sticks, and it felt even better to watch her chew on a strand of her own hair.

"I'm not working today," Mama had told me that morning soon after Daddy left. "So bring home a quart of milk after school."

When Theron was here, she brought home a gallon every few days from Shaw's, where she worked. But now that he was gone, even a quart went sour before we used it up. Mama used to say we went through so much milk that we should buy a cow and put her in the backyard, but she never said that anymore.

"Don't stop along the way—and you know what I mean," she told me as she handed me a five-dollar bill. Mama could smell the river and knew if I have been near that water.

I knew exactly what she meant. Buying milk gave me a reason to walk down along the river, my magic place. Something about the river, especially in spring when it rippled and ran high, pulled me toward it, and I couldn't ever walk by it without paying a visit. I'd tell myself, *You just keep going,* but before I knew, I'd be walking down the path in back of the library to the sandy beach, and tugging off my sneakers and socks and rolling up my jeans past my knees. Then I sat on the big, flat rock fixed halfway into the water.

The rocks at the bottom were furry and you had to be careful where you stepped or you'd slip. But the water was clear and quiet in the shallow places — the only places I would go — and the rocks trapped all kinds of things. Once I found a tiny gold ring with a deep green stone and swirls etched into the gold band. When I first found it, I could wear it on my pinkie, but then it got too small to squeeze my finger through. Now it was in my music box, the one with the broken ballerina that Mama say I got on my first birthday — though I was too young to remember — along with a necklace I got for my sixth birthday and the things I didn't put on the collage. Sometimes when I looked at that ring, I'd wonder if the baby who lost it was still searching for it. Or even if she knew she ever had such a pretty ring to lose.

Sometime after I couldn't fit the ring on my finger anymore, and before Theron left, I asked Mama, "What would you do if I got lost?"

"I would spend the rest of my life looking for you," she say. That from Mama made me feel cared about.

When I went down the path to the river that day, what I found was that new girl, Meadow Lark Frankenfield, sitting on my rock and dabbling her feet in the water.

She looked up with her good eye and her

popped-out eye and smiled at me, but I had to blink and look away. I just wasn't used to her face yet.

"This is my place, and that's my rock," I say without looking at her. And definitely without smiling.

"Really?" Meadow Lark asked, and out of the corner of my eye I saw her looking around. "I don't see the sign."

"Sign?"

"The one that says 'Keep Off River Rose Byrne's Rock.'"

That took the pepper out of my pants, and I asked, "How do you know my name?" If she knew my whole name, I wondered what else she knew about me.

"Well, it's hardly a secret," she say, but she didn't budge from where she sat on the rock. Instead she kicked up a curl of water. I watched the ripples slide away with the current.

"Where did you come from?" I asked.

"Phoenix. Do you know where that is?"

"I know where it is." Well, I knew it was a star on a map somewhere in the west, farther away than Texas, where red mountains and blue sky happened every day. And just so she wouldn't ask me if I knew exactly where, I stepped closer to the rock, hoping it would make her move off. But Meadow Lark just kept kicking the river, churning it up with her feet, stirring up the soft stuff that grew on the bottom.

"Stop mucking up the water like that."

She surprised me when she stopped, and that made me start to like her.

"Rivers are nice," she say. "Is that how you got your name?"

I shrugged. "Maybe. It's the name my mama gave me."

"I didn't have a river in Phoenix. And I don't have a mama. You're lucky. You have both."

I walked a few steps upstream from her and took off my sneakers and rolled up my jeans. Then I held my breath against the cold water and stepped in only until my toes were covered, and crouched.

"But that was my other mama," I say, flattening my palms against the surface of the river. "I'm adopted."

"Then you have a river and two mamas."

"Well . . . I don't know anything about my first one, and no one lets me ask about her, so I just consider that I have one."

Meadow Lark got off the log and come and crouched next to me. "Since I have none, then maybe you understand a little how I feel." In the sun her pumpkin-colored hair looked more carrot.

I did understand how she felt, being new and not having a mama, so I hoped she wouldn't mind if I asked her a personal question. "How can you see out of that eye?"

When she laughed, I knew it was okay.

"My glasses help," she say, "but sometimes I have to squint. And if I get tired, outlines get blurry and separate into colors."

"You mean like a prism?"

"I guess you could say that I have my own prism." She kept looking into the water. "I could have an operation to fix it, but I'm sick of operations."

I wanted to ask her about those operations, but by the thin way she answered, I decided to tuck my questions away for later.

"One time I found a bone right here," I say. "It looked like a squirrel bone, and it had a BB in it."

"Really?" she say, now drawing slow figure eights in the water. Something else, not bones with BBs in them, was on her mind, and she asked suddenly, "Why does Daniel Bunch talk to you like that?"

Right away I felt my back stiffen up. "Like what?"

"Like he knows a secret about you."

I shrugged and reached for a green-and-white stone through the water. "Daniel talks to everybody like that." My neck started to prickle, and the prickling crawled up my scalp.

"No, he doesn't," she say, and stopped drawing.

Now my face burned, not because Daniel Bunch talked like that to me, but because Meadow Lark had noticed that he did. It was the same feeling I had when she sat with me on the bench after she'd seen Daniel talking to me. I didn't want her—or anyone— seeing that.

I splashed a handful of water on my face to cool off. "I do this all the time," I say so she wouldn't know I was embarrassed again. "Since you know all about me, you tell me the secret."

"I didn't say there was a secret, but just that he acts like there's one."

"You know he's the one started that name about you."

Then she stepped out of the water and sat on the sand with her legs straight out in front, and tied her hair into a knot. "I've been called lots of names before—Popeye, Hunchback, Frankenstein—but Frankenfemme's the most creative."

"But doesn't it hurt when they say things like that?"

Meadow Lark Frankenfield shrugged. "Not most of the time. I have more important things to do."

Anyone who wasn't afraid of Daniel Bunch was someone I wanted to know. I stepped out of the water and sat W next to Meadow Lark.

"You can do that too? Look," Meadow Lark say, and bent her legs same way, with her calves at her sides and ankles pointed out.

"My parents keep telling me not to, but I can't sit crisscross, like most kids can."

"Me neither," Meadow Lark say, and pressed her knees flat onto the sand. "Crisscross hurts."

Maybe the new girl and I had more in common than liking Cheetos. Even her popped-out eye didn't surprise me anymore. It had become the way Meadow Lark looked. Then I realized there was more pretty about her than just her name.

"You want to walk along the shore?" she asked, looking downriver. "Maybe we'll find something there."

I shook my head. "We can't. I'm not even supposed to be *here*."

"So what's down there?" she asked.

I picked up some sand and let it run through my curled-up fist. "Just . . . we're not supposed to go there."

"Doesn't that make you want to?"

"No. You're really, really not supposed to go there. Besides, the best things from the river stop right here. I found some glasses and a tiny plastic doll, and once I found a silver dollar."

A dragonfly hovered over the water and glided through the air toward us. Meadow Lark shrieked and sprang up from the sand. "I hate dragonflies!"

It was so funny to see a girl who was not afraid of Daniel Bunch running around and waving her arms and screaming over a dragonfly. Finally it swooped away, and she stepped back to the shore and peered into the water.

Then two thoughts come to me. One: How could a person who wasn't afraid of Daniel Bunch be afraid of a beautiful dragonfly? And two: I was a lot like Meadow Lark — no better and no worse — because we were both afraid of something. That's when I began to hope that Meadow Lark Frankenfield would be my friend.

"I found a skull in the desert," Meadow Lark say. "Not a human one — it was a lizard. Now it's on my dresser in my new house. What did you do with everything you found here?"

"Most of them are on my collage at school."

"I wish I could find something today," she say, reaching into the water, "like this."

Meadow Lark pulled up a yellow bead shaped like a flower. "Here," she say, and dropped it into my palm, where it sparkled with water and sand.

"Pretty," I say, and handed it back to her.

But she shook her head. "It's yours," she say, and looked back into the water.

"Thanks," I say. *It would be perfect for my collage,* I thought, and tucked it deep into my pocket.

"I think," Meadow Lark say, "all those things landed here just for you, because they knew you like to come here."

Maybe it had to do with her eye, but Meadow Lark had a different way of seeing. But I shrugged and say politely, "Maybe."

Then she pointed upriver to where it curved and made a sandbar. "Let's go out there. I bet there are lots of treasures stuck in those rocks."

I looked at where she was pointing. To get to the sandbar, you had to walk in the water up to your knees, at least, and I couldn't do that. "Y-you can go," I say, sloshing the water with my toes.

She waded out into the river until the water reached the middle of her calves. "Come on out," she called, and when I shook my head, she say, "Are you scared? I'll come get you."

"No, I'll . . . keep looking here."

"Whatever you want," she say. "But it's just a little water." Then she waded over to the sandbar and peered into the river.

Beside the chocolate bits was a jar of flour, and then I turned and saw a room beyond the pantry, on the other side of the kitchen. This brand-new room smelled like leather and the forest. It had a high ceiling and a big, solid table with birds and vines carved into its sides. Three legs fanned out beneath the table, planted on an Oriental rug that was deep red, with green and orange and brown and a milk-colored white woven into it, and fringed all around the edge. A dark wooden desk gouged with pencil marks and scratches sat against the wall, and a shelf with wooden slots stood on top, stuffed with envelopes and rolled-up papers. An old adding machine also sat on the desk, and I punched a few of its keys. Two tall windows side by side looked onto a sun porch, and a radiator—the kind with pipes—sat below them. Another doorway led back to the kitchen.

Just as I began to step through that door, Meadow Lark say, "It's getting cold," and I was back at the river.

Meadow Lark stood nearby, shivering. She wrapped her arms around herself, and goose bumps dotted her arms. The shadows from the trees on the other side reached across, and the chill licked my wet feet. It was time to go, but my hands were empty. I had nothing from the water except the yellow flower bead that Meadow Lark gave me.

"Maybe next time we'll find something else,"

Meadow Lark say, as if she knew exactly what I'd been thinking.

I liked that there would be a next time, but just so she wouldn't expect to find silver dollars and gold rings every time, I told her, "I only find something good every once in a while."

"Maybe you need to look harder."

And just as she say that, something fluttered on the sand near the rock — a feather as white as a baby's eye and shorter than my thumb.

I set it in my palm and held it out to Meadow Lark. "Here, you keep it," I say, and noticed for the first time that her eyes were the same color brown as the river bottom when the sun shone on it.

"No, you found it, so it's yours," she say, waving it away.

Just then, a puff of breeze lifted the feather off my hand, and I grabbed for it. But it was too quick and darted off.

"Over there," Meadow Lark say, pointing to a bush. She couldn't run very fast on her slow leg, so I dashed ahead of her. The feather had caught in a bush, but just as I got close, it fluttered off, and then again, always out of my reach. I followed it around the bend, and then stopped when the old covered bridge come into view, dark and menacing in the green of the woods. I saw the bank leading to its mouth and tall weeds growing on what used to be a path.

The feather quivered on a branch just a few feet away, teasing. I was already too close to the bridge, and the murky sight of it was enough to plant dread in my stomach. I grabbed for the feather and pinched it in my fingers. Then I carried it back to the beach and showed Meadow Lark.

"It's a perfect feather," she say, looking close. "It's the kind you make a wish on."

"You want to wish on it?" I asked, watching the feather flutter in my hand.

"Let's both make a wish, at the same time. Ready?" She crossed her fingers and squeezed her eyes shut. "One-two-three—go."

I'd already made my wish the night before, so I watched Meadow Lark's lips move to hers. When she was finished, she opened her eyes and asked, "All done?"

"I didn't make a wish."

"Then go ahead."

I shook my head. "No, I want to save my wishes."

"Save them for what?"

"Until I really need them," I say. "Let's just send it off now, okay?"

"River, what's the matter?" Meadow Lark asked.

What was the matter was always the same—Theron. I'd wished for more than two months for him to come back, and he hadn't. All the talk about wishes and miracles was just talk. What good would it do to wish on a feather?

But all I say was, "Nothing. I just don't know the wish rules."

"There aren't any rules. It's just a game."

"So go ahead and blow it away."

Meadow Lark shook her head. "No, you float it on the river."

"I never heard of that. Did you just make it up?"

"That's what they do where I come from."

"Where you come from?" I asked, puzzled. "I thought you didn't have a river in Phoenix."

"Well . . . ," she say slowly, "I've lived in lots of places. And in the other places—not Phoenix—that's what we did. I can't believe you've never heard of it."

"We must be slow," I say, and glanced at the feather ruffling in the light breeze. It looked alive.

"Sure you don't want to make a wish first?" she asked.

"Oh, okay, I'll make a silly little wish." That way, I figured, I wouldn't be disappointed when nothing come of it.

"No, you have to make a big, crazy wish that

you'd never, ever believe would come true. It has to be so big and crazy that it hurts to make and would break your heart if it didn't come true."

Too many hearts were already broken over Theron, so I thought of something else that could be big and crazy. Then I looked at Meadow Lark. "Okay, I have one."

"Remember, make it big and crazy," she say.

I closed my eyes and made my wish. *I want to know my real mama.*

When I opened my eyes, Meadow Lark say very seriously, "Now we put it in the water."

It was such a pretty feather, pretty enough to keep, pretty enough to put in your pocket as a lucky feather. It would be a shame to waste it down the river. "Sure you don't want to hold on to it?" I asked.

She shook her head and took the feather from me. "No, it has to carry those wishes away."

Then Meadow Lark stepped into the river up to her knees, out far enough for the current to carry our wishes a long way. She set the feather on the surface, and the river snatched it and whisked it off.

I watched the feather slide and twirl on the water until I couldn't see it anymore, letting my big, crazy, silly wish about my mama last only as long as I could see the feather. After it was gone, I wished I'd tucked that pretty feather in my pocket, so I could keep it in my ballerina box next to my emerald ring.

The pink light of dusk hung in the air when I got home, and as soon as I stepped inside and smelled onion casserole, I remembered the milk.

"Did you forget something, River?" Mama asked me, her hands planted on her hips and her mouth a straight line. "Just when I was at my last drop. Now I'll have to go out. Where . . ." She stopped and sniffed the air. "You've been down at the river. What have we told you about that?"

I nodded. "I'm sorry. I just forgot about the milk."

"Forgot? Get upstairs and stay there till I call you down," she say, unhooking her pocketbook from the rack by the door. "Think about what it means to be dependable."

"Where's Daddy?" I asked. It was dusk and he wasn't home yet from Boston.

"Don't change the subject."

I went upstairs, like Mama say, and tried to think about being dependable, but instead I fell asleep. Sometime later their voices woke me up, and then I heard Daddy's footsteps coming up the stairs and a soft knock on my door.

"River?"

I slid my bedspread halfway over my nose and I closed my eyes. The door opened slowly. Daddy come and sat on the bed and put his hand on the bedspread, where my ankle was, and jiggled it.

"Wake up, River. It's past eight. You have to eat."

I fluttered my eyelids, pretending to wake up, and mumbled, "Is it morning already?"

"No, it's already nighttime."

I rubbed my eyes and brushed the hair off my face. "I told Mama I was sorry about the milk, but she send me up here anyway."

"You have to be gentle with her. You know she's like a piece of glass these days," Daddy say. "And," he say with a little squeeze on my ankle, "remember to correct yourself when you talk."

"*Sent.* I'm trying, but I forget."

"I understand," he say, and smiled gently.

I yawned and then say, "I wish I knew how to make Mama happy again."

Daddy looked down at his hand on my ankle, and I noticed for the first time since Theron left how the skin of his cheeks folded like draperies beside his mouth. "Me too, honey."

Then a thought come to me, as if it walked in the door and sat on the bed with us. "Maybe what make—makes—her happy now is being sad. And being sad is the way she'll always be from now on."

Daddy squeezed my ankle again. "I sure hope that's not true."

He sat there on my bed while the wind-up clock they gave me last birthday ticked. I counted forty-three ticks. When my stomach growled, I realized the only thing I'd eaten since breakfast was half an apple—and none of Meadow Lark's pretzel sticks.

"Are you sure it's safe to go downstairs?" I asked.

"Mmm-hmm," Daddy say, and raised one eyebrow. "But if she starts to hum, let her sing."

At that moment I'd have given anything—even my emerald ring—to hear Mama hum again.

Chapter 4

That Sunday, as Mama and I sat in church—holy hot dogs!—my stomach started growling again.

"Shh!" Mama say, keeping her eyes on the altar. This was her sacred time.

My stomach felt stuck to the back of the pew, I was so hungry, and all I could think about was the stack of blueberry pancakes waiting at Doby's and the little bottles of syrup all lined up at each table. So I pressed my hands over my stomach and hunched over to muffle the noise, wondering if that little cube of bread about to come around on the silver tray could keep it quiet until lunchtime.

Mama flickered her eyes at me as a warning. She never let me go to Sunday school. She say Sunday school was a waste of good time for a girl like me, so ever since I was old enough to remember, I come into church with her and Daddy and Theron. These days Daddy stayed until the offering plates started passing across the pews, and then he slipped to the side and out the back door. He say the Cathedral of Nature was the only church he cared to attend anymore.

"Pay attention," Mama say. It was what she always say to me whenever communion began and a hush as heavy as whipped cream filled the sanctuary. While other kids had doodle pads to keep them quiet, I wasn't allowed. I had to sit up straight with my ears perked and eyes wide open. If ever there was a time to pay attention, Mama say, it was during communion. While Pastor talked about the body, and then broke the loaf of bread in two, Mama stared straight at him. "Keep your eyes on that bread," she always say when he broke it, "because that's when you might see the truth."

"The truth of what?" I always ask, but she always just shushes me.

Sometimes I think she meant Jesus, after he come back to life and ate with his friends. I haven't seen him yet. Haven't seen him in the stained glass behind the communion table, haven't heard him in the flapping of bulletins, or smelled him in the breath of prayers around me. Haven't ever sensed a glow of him crouched in the murky space beside the pulpit. When I asked Mama if she ever saw the truth during communion, she say, "Not yet."

But I learned that, for Mama, that's what hope is—the moment just before the bread breaks or when dusk falls. It's the moment she holds her breath and waits to see with her eyes what her heart longs for.

After service, Mama stopped to talk to Pastor, so I threaded my way through the crowd and went outside to find Daddy. Before Theron left, Daddy often stood on the grass with the other men. Like Daddy, they wore pastel-colored shirts. Like Daddy, the smell of their aftershaves floated on the breeze. And like Daddy, they belonged to the Cathedral of Nature, the Church of Fishing, and the Fellowship of Barbecue. But these days he was usually in the car, reading the paper or listening to the ball game or thumb-tapping the steering wheel waiting for Mama and me to finish.

I was never sure if it was their choice or his that he be in the car by himself instead of with the men, but I knew it had something to do with Theron and what everyone say he'd done. I hoped it wasn't the men's decision to leave Daddy out, because church— like family—was supposed to be a place to forgive.

After I left Mama, I went out to the parking lot to look for him. Today he wasn't in the car, but then I looked across the lawn and saw Daddy standing with the other men.

It had begun to rain a fine mist that drifted like fog, the kind of drizzle that started off soft and steady but hinted at days and days of rain to come. I stepped carefully on the grass to keep from sinking into the moist earth.

As I got closer to Daddy, he reached out his arm to touch me as soon as he could. All the time it took me to reach him, he didn't stop looking at the other men as they talked. Usually they leaned back and laughed or put their hands in their pockets, or slapped their thighs. But today, by the way they stood like a grove and crossed their arms over their chests or leaned in to one another, or rubbed their cheeks or pulled their chins, I knew this conversation was of a serious nature.

I ran into Daddy's arm, and when he wrapped it around me, I tried hanging off him.

"How big are you now?" Mr. Clapton asked. He had one tooth that stuck out, even when his mouth was closed.

"Eleven."

"Well, you're way too big to hang now. You're almost in high school."

I looked at Daddy, who shrugged at me, and then back at Mr. Clapton. I remembered he didn't have any kids, and decided he didn't know how old you had to be in high school. Also, Mama say he'd had a hard life and relied on his community for help, and that we needed to be good neighbors.

"Almost," I say, to be polite. Then I whispered to Daddy, "Mama's dying for Doby's."

"Mama?" he say, and raised his eyebrow. He put his finger to his lips, not like Mama in church, but as if to say, *Wait a little bit, until we're done talking.* Whenever Daddy talked to me like that, I had trouble believing I ever heard him raise his voice to Theron.

"I'm telling you," Mr. Mittell, Sonya's daddy, say, "we're in for a flood this year. Watch the rain, watch the bridges. You remember that summer—"

"Rain didn't swell the river that summer, Vin," Daddy say. "It was snow melt."

"It was rain, Ingram," Mr. Clapton say to Daddy, though he looked at me. "The same year the old bridge flooded and you—"

"No," Daddy say, very short. I felt his arm tighten, and he shook his head like a muscle twitch, as if to tell Mr. Clapton to stop talking.

The covered bridge? I wondered.

"If you hadn't been on the bridge to save them . . . ," Mr. Clapton say, and then glanced at me without another word. By the way Daddy had tensed up and cut Mr. Clapton off, I knew better than to ask what he meant. So I just waited for Mr. Clapton to open his mouth, to see if all his teeth were crooked.

Daddy waved away the conversation. "That was the past. It's all over with," he say, and then I knew that Daddy had a secret.

"It can happen again," Mr. Mittell say, looking up at the gray sky. "The rain's already started." Then he looked straight at me. "And you, young lady, you stay off the bridges."

After Daddy and I moved away from the men and went looking for Mama, I asked, "What were they talking about?"

But all he say was, "Did someone say something about pancakes?"

On the fourth Sunday of each month, Mama takes flowers to the family. She piles all the gardening equipment into the trunk—spades, gardening gloves, the big metal watering pot, and a cardboard box lid with the flowers she bought at Pike's Nursery the day before—and then lets Daddy take over until we arrive at the Green Memorial Cemetery.

Every time before we go, she say, "River, take that watering can outside and run the hose through it." There's usually a spider or two that made a home in that can since the month before, but sometimes it's worse. Two years ago I found a dead mouse. Daddy set it aside and Theron and I buried it later behind the stone-wall fence because I felt sad for it.

But this Sunday there was only one spider. Not a big, hairy one, but a daddy longlegs. They don't really qualify as spiders because I'm not afraid of them. This one was still alive, and I let it walk up my arm before lowering it to the grass.

Mama stopped driving after Theron left us. She say it was like a hunger strike, but Daddy grumbled that the only person affected was everyone else. Meaning him, who had to drive her everywhere she couldn't walk to. I think Theron was just an excuse, because by the time she stopped driving, she had put dents in both sides of the back bumper, sliced off the side-view mirror on a mailbox, and driven off the road more than three times in the same month.

Just after Theron left, Mama was driving us to Concord when a thunderstorm hit. In three seconds the highway turned into a pond. Daddy told her to slow down. I had a bag of pretzel sticks in my lap and was about to put a pretzel in my mouth when the car wiggled and spun around, and then it took off and slid clear across the highway.

I watched Daddy's hands grip the dash until all his

knuckles turned pink and, when he was sure nothing worse was going to happen, heard the breath wobble out of him. Later, Mama say that I screeched so loud she thought we'd hit a clowder of cats, and I didn't stop screaming until we come to rest a foot from the cement divider wall.

Nothing hit us, and we didn't hit anything, we didn't flip over, and no one got hurt. We spun around and around and stopped, facing in the right direction. That's when I remembered my pretzels, but when I put one in my mouth, I poked a hole in my cheek because my hand shook so.

As Daddy's breathing come back to normal, Mama stared straight out the windshield. "What did I tell you?" she say. "Angels."

After Mama loaded the trunk that Sunday after church, she left it open until Daddy inspected it to make sure everything was there so we wouldn't have to turn back once we got to the cemetery. Then we all climbed into the car. Even with the sprinkling rain, there were no exceptions to going to the family. We had ponchos and umbrellas if the sprinkles turned into a downpour.

Beside me in the backseat was that empty yawn where Theron would have sat. He'd be sitting behind

Mama because Daddy had to push his own seat back and Theron's legs were too long.

We drove through town and along the lonely two-lane road that eventually ran into the highway. Daddy turned the car onto the narrow gravel road, and the tires crunched all the way to the little hill in the shade, near the faucet that poked out of the ground. Some of the headstones had little flags beside them, others had flowers, and those without either looked left out.

While Daddy carried the box lid full of flowerpots and I filled the watering can, Mama put on her visor and slipped on her gloves. Then she took the spades over to the family headstones and started digging.

Mama planted flowers according to the season. In summer she planted pots of phlox and daylilies, in fall she planted asters and chrysanthemums, in winter she brought arrangements of grasses and leaves and twigs, and in spring she planted pink impatiens and crocuses and columbines for the family. And she always brought more than we needed, and dropped off the leftovers at the hospital, where she used to volunteer, a few miles down the road.

Today she carried a box of daffodils, a flower that bloomed in the seam of spring and summer. Also because it was Grampa Raymond's favorite flower.

By now Daddy was done with his part of the job, and he sat in the car with the door open and one foot flat on the ground. The ball game was on the radio, and the announcer's sharp voice cut into the cemetery quiet.

"Bring some water over here, River," Mama say after she patted down the dirt around Grampa's flowers. I lugged the can over to her, trying to keep the water from sloshing out.

She sat back on her heels and wiped her forehead with her arm. "You remember your Grampa Raymond, don't you?"

I looked at the headstone. Nothing about it helped me remember my grampa. "I remember his cheeks were scratchy."

"Well, you were just a baby—I mean, just a little girl," Mama say, as if she'd forgotten I didn't come to them until I was almost two.

"Well, he lay asleep for a week, and your grandma thought he was gone. Suddenly, he sat straight up and opened his eyes wide, like he heard a thunderclap, and said, 'There they are, Mother.' And then he lay back down and closed his eyes."

"What did he see?"

"We don't know, because right after that he was gone," she say, and leaned forward onto her knees again and finished patting down the dirt, though it already looked perfect to me. "But Grandma thought he might have seen . . . people."

I knew Mama meant angels because she believed in them, but she say, "We'll never know."

She planted three flowers for every stone in the family, which was four—plus the big one that the two sets of great-grandparents shared—and there was always one extra flowerpot in the box lid.

"There," Mama say, and brushed off her hands. We were done for the month. She gathered up the spades and her gloves and pushed herself up. "Pick up the extra one, honey."

I lifted the box with the last daffodil pot in it and followed Mama a few yards to June R. Wadleigh's stone. June R. Wadleigh was a family friend, and her stone sat far enough away to respect the family boundaries but close enough to peek in its windows.

Mama got to work digging up last month's flower and putting in the daffodil. As always, after she dropped the new flower in the hole, she say to me, "Now you fill in the dirt and pat it down."

When I finished, Mama sprinkled the last of the water on June R. Wadleigh's daffodil. Then she handed me the spades and gloves. "Take these back to the car. I'll be there soon."

That's what usually happened every time we went to the family. Mama told me to go on to the car, and then Daddy and I packed up while Mama stayed behind a few minutes, tidying up everything one last time before we left.

Daddy stepped out of the car. I followed him to the trunk, and as he took the box from me, I glanced beyond him and saw Mama with her hand on June R. Wadleigh's stone. What she did look so familiar, but also so new. It seemed like I noticed for the very first time that Mama always spent the last moments of each visit with June R. Wadleigh.

"Move that for me, will you?" Daddy say, pointing his chin at a bag of books inside the trunk. I knew a distraction when I heard one.

"Daddy, why does Mama always touch that stone before we go?" I asked, clearing a space for the watering can.

"That stone? Well, your mama felt very close to June."

Mama pushed her hair off her face and started walking back to the car, so I had to talk as fast as possible. "You mean close like best friends?"

He looked over his shoulder, in Mama's direction, and then back at me. "River, you're almost in high school, right?" he asked and winked, though there was no smile on his face. I didn't know why he was pretending to move things around in the trunk when everything already fit. Then he leaned against the taillight and his eyes looked very sad.

"They were close like sisters."

That was all Daddy say, but from that little bit I learned something new about Mama. That she, too, have a secret.

We got into the car. Daddy turned down the volume on the baseball game before Mama had to tell him to, and we left until next month. All the way home I thought about what Daddy had told me about Mama's friend June. Mama once had a best friend as close to her as a sister.

Meadow Lark was becoming my friend. We both had something to be afraid of and we both sat W and we both liked Cheetos. She gave me a yellow flower bead, and we floated that perfect feather with our wishes down the river. I hoped that she and I, like Mama and June, could become best friends just like sisters.

Chapter 5

"This came out of my grampa's mouth," Daniel Bunch say, as he waved his hand right in front of my face. I knew what it was—a molar with a silver filling in it—but I made a point of not looking at it.

We sat at big butcher-block tables in art class, eight kids at a table, on stools that teetered and thudded. The tables were big enough that we could spread out our collages. I set mine longways in front of me so it wouldn't touch anyone else's, especially Daniel Bunch's. Daniel sat across from me. I don't know why Ms. Zucchero sat us at the same table, because she had to know that something with one eye open slept between us.

"That's so *interesting*," Sonya Mittell say. Sonya had worn a bra in fourth grade, and she needed to. Then kids started calling her Sonya Barbie, but not for long, because she liked it.

"Brave guy, nerves of steel," Kevin Kale say, sitting kitty-corner to me.

Normally, when kids talk too much, Ms. Zucchero gave a warning. But maybe because it was Friday, or art was last period today, or the school year was almost over, she only say, "When your collage is done, please tack it to the wall."

Ms. Zucchero's hands were always holding something—carrots or paintbrushes or fabric. Today she held a crochet hook that went in and out of a green square speckled white. She wound the yarn around her finger and plunged the needle back into the square. She usually finished one square during each class. Ms. Zucchero told us that when all the squares were done, she was going sew them all together to make a blanket for next winter.

"My grampa hated dentists," Daniel say, because he knew Kevin's daddy was a dentist. The air coming from Daniel's way smelled like bacon grease.

I squeezed a blob of glue onto my collage, next to the porcelain doll head with no nose, and set the bottle in front of me.

Daniel snapped his fingers. "Glue," he say, and I slid the bottle to the center of the table. As I did, I saw what else he had on his collage. A stick with a dirty string wound around it, a Twinkie wrapper, some coins, and a jagged chunk of rock that he say come from a meteor.

If our collages were supposed to tell a story, the story Daniel Bunch's told was "What I Picked Up on My Way to School This Morning." That rock looked no different from one you'd find balancing on a sewer grate after a storm. Nobody at our table told Daniel it was everyday cement from the curb, though that's what everybody was thinking.

When I saw all those ordinary things Daniel had on his collage, it made me think he wasn't the wolf he wanted me to believe he was. He was more like a rat hiding from the wolf. A dirty stick with a string wrapped around it and a Twinkie wrapper, a tarnished nickel, and a rock from the street wouldn't catch a wolf's eye. Those were things a rat would stuff in its nest. Then he labeled everything with that rat-scratch scrawl of his that looked like it was written with a claw.

"My grampa's tough. He didn't even use anestesia," Daniel say.

Anes-thee-*sia*, I thought, spreading the glue with my finger. Then, before I could stop myself, I asked him, "You mean, he pull that tooth out himself?"

Daniel stopped talking. Everyone stopped talking. Stopped cutting, gluing, pressing, breathing.

He stared at me. "You eavesdropping?" he say very normal so that Ms. Zucchero wouldn't hear, but I felt his threat closing around my throat.

I shook my head.

"You better not. Not listening, not looking."

"Eavesdropping is *rude*," Sonya say in that voice of hers as thin as plastic wrap, and she looked at Daniel like *Now do you like me?*

Daniel say, "Now she'll whine to big brother that I was mean to her," and then bumped his head with his fist. "Forgot—big brother isn't here. Because he couldn't keep his car on the road."

That was the hardest part to hear about that night—that Theron was drunk when he drove into the river with Daniel in the car.

"And if he ever comes back, they'll electrocute him," Sonya say.

"Zzzap-Zap!" Daniel say, and clutched his hand over his heart, like he was shocked.

Kevin laughed. He was afraid of Daniel. In fourth grade Daniel punched him every morning before school started, because Daniel didn't like that Kevin got all As.

My eyes stung, but I blinked back the tears and say, "My brother didn't do anything wrong. He leave because—"

"He's a wimp," Daniel say.

"What kind of accent is that, anyway?" Sonya asked. "I can't sleep trying to figure it out."

"It's called fake," Daniel say, and blew on his collage. His bacon-grease smell drifted across the table at me. "Don't let her fool you."

"It's funny she never used to talk like that. She used to talk like us," Sonya say.

My face felt so hot and my neck prickled. The clock above Ms. Zucchero's desk say almost two-fifteen. Then the bell would ring, and school would be over, and I could leave. I dropped the yellow flower bead that Meadow Lark gave me into the glue on my collage. The bead was the last thing I wanted to put on it. Grains of sand had tucked deep among the flower petals, and when I stopped pressing, the petals left a pink-and-white imprint on my fingertip. In a few minutes the glue would be dry.

"River reminds me of the way my grandfather from the low country talked," Ms. Zucchero say. "I haven't heard my granddaddy's voice for a long, long time."

I blew on my collage to hide my smile. Ms. Zucchero had come as a replacement teacher in April, a few weeks after Theron left. I wondered—would she be as nice to me if she knew what Theron did? If she knew what they say he did—that he was drunk and drove Daniel into the river?

The glue was almost clear now, making the collage almost done. No one at my table was talking anymore, because nobody wanted to tell a better story than the one about Daniel's molar or the rock from a meteor. When I tapped the glue once more around the flower bead, it felt dry. So I hopped off the chair and started to pick my collage off the table, being careful that it didn't touch anyone else's, especially Daniel's.

"Wait," Sonya say, and looked around the table. "What does everyone think of her collage? She worked so hard on it."

I thought Sonya was trying to be nice after what Ms. Zucchero say, so I held up my collage.

Daniel looked at it like he was inspecting a gold ring, and then he say, "It stinks."

I held my collage in both hands, and suddenly what I had found in the river wasn't all that special anymore. It just looked like a bunch of junk dumped onto the shore. That collage for Mama stunk, Daniel say, but I didn't have enough time to change it.

I took some tacks from the Maxwell House coffee can on the bookshelf and pinned my collage to the wall. When Daniel Bunch come up beside me and

tacked up his collage, the muscles in my back tight-
ened up.

"Something's missing," he muttered, "Something . . ."

He must be talking about his sad collage, I thought, and
went back to the table to clean up. I brushed the scraps
of colored paper and tape into my hand. I wet a paper
towel and rubbed off the glue where I'd sat at the table.
And just as I threw the paper towel into the big trash
bin, Meadow Lark come into the room carrying a vase
with a grip of pink carnations in it.

"The office sent me," she say.

"How pretty," Ms. Zucchero say, and smiled.
"Who are they from?" There was a rumor that she
had a crush on Mr. Sievers, the music teacher, and
maybe she hoped they were from him. I hoped they
were.

"There's a card," Meadow Lark told her.

Maybe the rumor was true, because when she
read the card, Ms. Zucchero say, "Oh, they're from
my brother," in a voice plain as chewed gum.

Meadow Lark's face looked so solemn, as if she
too had hoped the flowers were from Mr. Sievers, so
I smiled at her to cheer her up. But just then someone
whispered, "Frankenfemme," and it grew—"Frankenfemme, Frankenfemme"—until the name filled the
room like a hairy animal.

Meadow Lark didn't turn red or cry or even run out of the room. It was as if she didn't hear them. Instead her hands started to shake, and her good eye opened wide across her solemn face, and she say, "River, look!"

I turned around to see Daniel Bunch shaking a paintbrush at my collage, spattering black paint all over the things I'd saved, all over my gift for Mama.

"Daniel!" shouted Ms. Zucchero, as I dashed to the wall. I grabbed the paintbrush from him, but he held it tight, still shaking it at my collage. He spattered paint all over the yellow flower bead and the baby and the stone like a face and the key, the bear tooth—all over everything.

Daniel looked over his shoulder at Ms. Zucchero. "What—oh, this?" he say, with his eyebrows raised high, like he had no idea he was doing anything wrong. "It was an *accident*." But I knew exactly what he meant—just like the accident with Theron.

At that moment the final bell rang, and my feet began moving before I knew what they were doing or where they were taking me. They carried me out of the art room and out of the school, up the street to the library, and down the path to the river.

Meanwhile, my mind carried me to that house. I was in the big dining room with the carved table and the desk with the adding machine and the square shelves, and the doorway that led back to the kitchen. The house was building itself in front of me, spreading its rooms in front of me. I saw a staircase in the space between the dining room and kitchen, but it turned halfway up, so I couldn't see to the top.

I put my foot on the first step, when I heard, "River! Come back!" It was Meadow Lark, standing on the shore. She waved, and the breeze lifted her hair around her face like she was flying.

I was standing up to my calves in the river. "Meadow Lark!" I called, my legs paralyzed with fear and cold.

"Wait there," she called, and waded out to me and grabbed my hand. "Follow me," she say, and led me step by step all the way back to the sandy beach.

"What were you doing out there?" she asked.

"I don't know. I was just . . . What was I doing out there?" I asked, and sank to the ground. I buried my head in my arms and breathed. The rain falling on the water sounded like a zither.

"You were walking out into the middle of the river," she say. "That current could have swept you away."

I raised my head and watched the river slide by. That was the farthest I'd ever gone in there. What if I had gone even farther? What if—

"It's a good thing you come along when you did,"
I say.

Meadow Lark was drawing in the sand with
a twig. "You could have drowned—all because of
Daniel Bunch."

She understood how I felt. "I wish Daniel Bunch
was . . . I wish he would leave us alone." But that
wasn't all I wanted to say.

"That's what you want?" Meadow Lark asked.
"You want him to go away?"

"Sort of . . . don't you?" I asked, remembering
how her hand shook in the art room when they called
her Frankenſemme.

Without saying a word, she reached into her backpack and pulled out a pencil and a corner of lined
paper. Then she started writing something.

"What are you doing?" I asked.

"We're making a wish. See?" she say, and handed
the paper to me.

We wish Daniel Bunch would drop dead.

I took a sharp breath, because Meadow Lark
had written what I hadn't say. It was just like she
could read my mind. But seeing my wish on the
paper made me feel like throwing up. Wishing
Daniel Bunch to be dead ran a chill from my toes to
my scalp.

I pushed the paper back to her. "You have to change it to say 'disappear' instead."

Meadow Lark squinted at me through her glasses, and then crossed out *drop dead*.

"No," I say, "you have to erase it, or it'll still be in the wish."

"You're being really persnickety," she say, but she erased it and wrote: *We wish Daniel Bunch would disappear.*

We looked at each other and nodded. Then I found a peel of birch bark on the beach, near where the woods began, and Meadow Lark laid the wish on it.

"Now you need to take it far out, so it will float a long way," I say.

"One day you have to stop being afraid of the water."

"One day, I know," I say, and shivered. "But not today."

Meadow Lark took the birch bark and stepped into the river, out to where the current ran free and the water reached her knees, and set that wish down. That made three wishes we'd floated down the river. And I believed not one of them would come true.

The river took it swift. I fixed my eyes on that curl of bark until it turned into a speck and then a twinkle of broken sunlight. When I realized it was too late to take back the wish, that shiver went up my back again, and I rubbed my arms to stop shaking.

It was just a piece of paper with some writing on it, I knew, and Meadow Lark had erased part of it. The wish we'd written about Daniel Bunch, which was probably falling apart in the water that very moment, wasn't all that worried me. What worried me was the wish still in my heart, the one I didn't say. If only I could erase that one.

Meadow Lark stood in the river, looking downstream, for a few more minutes. Suddenly she pointed at something in the woods and called, "River, look over there—what is that?"

Chapter 6

I looked in the direction she was pointing and saw something white in the bushes. It seemed to wriggle. "It looks like a bunch of feathers," I say.

"Go over and take a look," she say, and started plowing her way back to shore.

I walked closer and saw that it was a bird, and it was caught in a bush. When he saw me coming, he raised his head and flapped at me, but only one wing opened all the way. The other stayed close to his body, as if it was broken. White feathers fluttered off his body and floated in the air. He was stuck in that bush.

"It's all right," I say to the bird and cupped my hands around his body. He blinked and cooed, and let me untangle him. As soon as I held him firm in my hands, he settled down, as if he had been waiting for someone to come along and rescue him. I stroked his head, and he cooed again and blinked.

Meadow Lark had returned to the beach by the time I come out of the woods.

"It's a pigeon or a dove," she say, and patted him. Then she put her face up to his. "Hey, pidge, you're cute."

He tilted his head, as if trying to figure her out.

"Something's wrong with his wing," I say, touching it gently. "It looks broken."

"We can't leave him here—there are wild animals in these woods. They could eat him in a split second."

"We have an old guinea-pig cage at home—we could put him in that."

"So you'll take him home?"

"Well, I don't know . . . my mama doesn't like birds. She say they're dirty and sly."

"She'll like this one. Who wouldn't like him?" Meadow Lark say, putting her face close to his again.

"My mama wouldn't. Why don't you take him?"

"My dad's allergic," she say very quickly, keeping her eyes on the bird. "He needs a name. Mr. Tricks is a perfect name."

"It's a funny name for a bird that doesn't do any tricks."

"Well, I had another Mr. Tricks. He . . . flew out of his cage and never came back, and I always wished I could have used the name longer."

"I guess that's one trick this bird can't do. Maybe he's faking his broken wing so he can go home with me," I say.

Meadow Lark laughed. "There's a good trick."

We left the river, taking turns carrying Mr. Tricks, and Meadow Lark walked with me as far as my house.

"So, this is where you live?" she say. "It's a good-looking house."

By then it was close to suppertime. "You want to stay for supper?" I asked.

"That depends—what are you having?"

"I don't know, but my mama's a good cook. She works at Shaw's, and sometimes she brings home a whole cooked dinner." I sniffed. "Maybe she brought home a roast chicken today."

Meadow Lark glanced at the house, then at Mr. Tricks. "Roast chicken? Maybe not this time."

We say good-bye and I went into the garage, holding Mr. Tricks in one hand while I rummaged around for the guinea-pig cage. I found it behind Mama's big suitcase, and dusted it off. Then I tore up some newspapers and put them in the bottom of the cage. I put Mr. Tricks in and latched the door closed. The last thing I needed was for him to get lost in our house, or worse, try to fly away with his broken wing.

I carried the cage to the porch. Mr. Tricks cooed the whole time. The front staircase was a few feet away on the other side of the screen door. I could see Mama, standing with her back to me in the kitchen at the end of the hallway. If I could just get in the house and up the stairs without her seeing me, we'd be safe for a while.

"*Shh*," I told Mr. Tricks, and slowly opened the screen door.

"River?" Mama say.

I kept quiet as I carried the cage to the staircase.

"River, is that you?"

"Yes, Mama," I say, halfway up the stairs.

"Where have you been?"

At the top of the stairs I say, "I'll be right down."

I tiptoed with the cage to my room and shut the door.

"Don't coo anymore," I say to Mr. Tricks, and set him on my bureau. Then I filled a lid with water and put it in his cage. That would have to do until I could bring up some bread and salad from supper.

I put my face up to the cage. "Hi, pidge," I say. Mr. Tricks tilted his head at me and blinked. Meadow Lark was right—he was cute.

Dusk was falling outside, and Mr. Tricks glowed like the moon in fog. I covered his cage with a towel so he'd think it was night and go to sleep. "Good night for now," I say.

He cooed at me in reply.

Then I washed up really well to get the river smell off me, and went downstairs, where I knew Mama would ask me all about where I'd been and what I'd been up to.

Chapter 7

It was raining again the next day when Meadow Lark showed up on our porch, her nose pressed flat against the screen door. Mama had just put Saturday-night supper on the table, and the smell of maple baked beans drifted out the open door.

"What are you doing here?" I asked quickly — because all that good smell was leaking through the screen.

"Can I come in?"

Mama called from the kitchen, "Who's at the door, River? It's suppertime."

Mama had strict rules about when you should visit another person's house, when you should call them on the phone — not before breakfast or after nine o'clock at night — and how to write a thank-you note.

"A girl from school," I called back. Mama didn't have to know everything about Meadow Lark that very second.

"What does she want? Is she fund-raising? I don't have much to give for fund-raising right now."

"No, she's not selling anything." I turned back to Meadow Lark. "Are you?"

"No," she say, and I heard Mama open the refrigerator door.

"Does your friend want to stay for supper?" Mama asked. "Bring her in before the food gets cold."

Through the blurry screen, Meadow Lark's good eye widened. "Can I? It smells so good."

I opened the door for her. "So, why are you here?" I whispered. I wanted her reason to be a good one, because seeing her made me happy. She had to see me at school, she saw me at the river by accident, but she appeared to come to my house on purpose.

"Well, because . . ." She looked behind her at the porch as if something out there waited for her. "Since you're my only friend here, I have to ask you—can I stay here?"

"Mama just invited you."

"No, I mean *stay* . . . like a sleepover, but for more than one night. My dad has to go out in the field for a while."

"What is he, a farmer?"

"He's a . . . geologist. I thought I told you that

before," she say, and looked around. "You have a nice house."

"Your daddy would let you stay here?"

"Uh-huh," she say, and nodded, making her hair bounce all around her. "I have to ask him, but I already know he'll let me because I've told him all about you. He won't go out in the field unless he knows I'm being taken care of by a good family. But if he doesn't go, he'll lose his job. And then we'll have to move again. So, can I?"

"Would you really move away?" I had just met her, and now that we were friends, I didn't want her to leave.

She nodded.

Mama would have so many reasons for why Meadow Lark would not be able to stay with us. It would change our routine, a person should wait to be invited, and Mama wouldn't want to be responsible for another person in the house. And when Theron come back, he might not like someone else here. Those would be Mama's minus reasons, but none of them were going to stop me from asking if Meadow Lark could stay.

"Wait here," I told Meadow Lark. "I'll ask."

I never had anyone stay overnight before. The time my cousins from Utica come for a long weekend, when I had to give them my bedroom and sleep on the rollaway in the living room, didn't count. They all smelled like their yellow Lab, Buster, and when they talked, they pronounced *R*s like they were squeezing the air out of them. Even Daddy sighed with relief when they packed up their car and left for home, with Buster hanging his head out the window.

But having Meadow Lark stay over would be a real sleepover. And Mama might not need much persuading today. Daddy was working all the way to Orlando and wouldn't be back for four days, and Mama liked having people around when he was gone. That would be a plus reason.

"First that bird and now a girl in your class" was her answer. "What will it be next?"

"No one, I promise."

"Who is this Meadow Lark? What do you know about her?"

I picked up a dish towel. "Well, she's from Arizona, and I'm her best friend."

"I'm glad you are," Mama say. I knew she worried that I didn't have any friends these days.

I wound the dish towel around my hand. "Please? She doesn't have any other place to go."

"What would she do if she can't stay here?"

"Her daddy won't be able to go out in the field,

and he'll lose his job, and then they'll have to leave their house."

I knew that, just like there was a rule in Mama's book that say you don't call after nine o'clock at night, there was another rule that say you don't turn your back on someone who needs your help. She had a tender place for strays and unattractive fruit that other people wouldn't choose, and I knew that tender place would include Meadow Lark.

"You'll have to clear off your other bed and share the bathroom," she say.

"I know." I tried hard to look calm, but inside I was doing jumping jacks.

"And it has to be okay with her father."

Then Mama turned to the counter to wipe it down, and I wrapped my arms around her. She didn't stop her wiping, but I felt her other hand cover mine in the same way she might protect a part of herself.

"Thank you, Mama. I love you," I say, and wished right then for a feather or a corner of lined paper. Wished I could look up at the sky and see a miracle come down for her. Wished she'd hum again in the kitchen.

Maybe Mama wished that too, because she squeezed my hand and whispered, "River, don't you ever forget what you mean to me."

When I got back to the hall, Meadow Lark stood up straight. "Can I?" I nodded, and we squeaked.

"We can get your stuff after supper," I say, but Meadow Lark waved that idea away. "I'll go by myself."

"Okay," I say, feeling disappointed. "And you have to ask your daddy."

"Of course."

So Meadow Lark come back after supper carrying her backpack, a leather duffel bag, a tote bag with ARIZONA sprawled across it like on a postcard, a Tupperware of something, and a bag of birdseed.

"For Mr. Tricks," she say, and set everything on the extra bed in my room.

She crouched down to his cage on the floor to take a look. "How is he doing?" Then she poked her finger through the bars. Mr. Tricks first settled in his usual way and tilted his head and blinked, but then he got up and strutted across the cage to her finger.

"That means he likes me," Meadow Lark say. "Has he done any tricks yet?"

"No, but I think his wing is better. When he ruffles himself, his bad wing come out a little more each time."

She sat on her bed. "My other Mr. Tricks was a parakeet. I got him after I came out of the hospital for the fourth time. He rode all the way to Arizona with us. One time he got out of the cage and hopped around the car until my dad made me put him back in."

This was the second time she talked about her operations, so this time I asked. "Why were you in the hospital?"

Meadow Lark put her finger up to the cage and looked at Mr. Tricks. "I don't really like to talk about that."

"Sorry," I say. "That was a bad start."

"It's okay. I just don't like operations. And I hate hospitals."

Then there was a long silence between us until I asked, "Did your parakeet poop in the car?"

At that she laughed and scrunched up her face. "He did! All down the back of my seat. My dad said he wouldn't drive another mile knowing *that* was in his car."

Mr. Tricks shook his head in a blur.

"There's a trick," she say. "He thinks we're talking about him." She clicked her tongue at him, and he cooed back.

"We have to remember one thing, though — Mama doesn't like birds, so we need to keep him in here all the time."

"She'll like Mr. Tricks. He grows on people." Meadow Lark always sounded so confident.

Then she reached into her backpack and pulled out an envelope. "Before I forget, this is for your parents. But you can read it too. It's from my dad."

Inside was a typewritten note on thin, crinkly paper. It read:

Dear Byrne family,

Thank you for letting my precious Meadow Lark stay with you while I'm working in the field. If you didn't, I could have lost my job. I should be gone only a few weeks. If anything happens, Meadow Lark knows how to contact me.

Yours truly,
Derek Frankenfield

"My dad has really bad handwriting, so he types everything," Meadow Lark explained before I could ask her.

"Mama will want his phone number too."

"I'll give it to her," she say, and pulled a wad of clothes from her duffel bag. "Where can I put these?"

I opened the bottom drawer of my bureau for her. "And you can have some space in my closet." Then I showed her the bathroom down the hall, and made room for her toothpaste, and showed her the towels I'd hung on the bar for her.

On our way back, she stopped in front of Theron's room and looked the door up and down. "Was this your brother's?"

"It *is* his room, but you can't go in. No one is allowed."

"I don't want to go in — I just want to look. Can I look, just for a minute?" she asked, and turned the doorknob so slowly that it didn't make a noise.

"I guess so," I whispered. "But be quiet."

Meadow Lark nudged the door open. All the usual things of Theron — his trophy, the bed made up with two pillows, one on top of the other, and his picture of Shawna on the bureau, were still there. The sunlight glowed through the gauze curtains, and I knew that before the day was over, Mama would come in and close the draperies, just like Theron would do every night if he were here.

"This is it," I say. "It's just like the day he left it."

"Kind of like a shrine." Meadow Lark took a few steps in. "Who is this?" she asked and reached for the picture of Shawna.

"Don't touch it! Come on, we have to get out."

"I just wanted to see," she say, but pulled her hand back. "Who is she?"

"That was his girlfriend. Well . . ." I wasn't even sure if she was. "He liked her."

"Really? Do you ever see her now?"

I shook my head. Shawna never come to see us after Theron left, and she never called. I saw her downtown a few times with some other girls from the high school. And once I saw her on her bicycle, but I ducked into the deli so I wouldn't have to talk to her.

Then Meadow Lark went over to the bed and sat on it so hard that it creaked.

"Don't do that!" I whispered as loud as I could without yelling, but she ignored me and spread her hand along the dark blue comforter.

"So, was he really drunk when he had the wreck?

"If we don't get out now — "

"Tell me and I'll get out. I promise." Then she leaned back on her arms, and for a second I thought she was going to lie down on Theron's pillows.

I crossed my arms over my chest and stood up straight and stiff. "Of course he wasn't drunk. Theron wouldn't do *anything* like that."

Meadow Lark say nothing for what seemed like a long time. She just kept smoothing her hand over Theron's comforter. Finally she say, "Innocent people don't leave. Tell me what happened."

My arms and legs felt like wet cardboard, so

shaky that I had to sit down in Theron's desk chair.

"Theron used to get into trouble all the time. It was awful then. So Daddy told him he was ruining our family, and if he mess up one more time, he'd have to go. That was about two years ago, when he was sixteen. Theron must have wanted to stay here, because then all the trouble stopped, and Daddy say he straightened up. But then the wreck happen."

I wanted to get that story out so fast that I didn't try to correct how I say it. But Meadow Lark never seemed to mind.

"And that was the one more time?"

I nodded. "Everyone say he was drunk. The night he crashed the car, he come right home. It was late and I was asleep, but I woke up when I heard Theron and Daddy arguing. They sound like they did before Theron straightened up. I couldn't hear all their words, but Daddy told him he had to go. He did not want Theron in this house anymore. He didn't yell it—he just sounded sad. And Theron say, 'Fine, I'm leaving. But I'm never coming back, so don't look for me.'"

Meadow Lark stopped touching the comforter and put her hands in her lap. "Wow, no wonder you miss him."

"So, you know about the wreck?" I asked.

Meadow Lark shook her head. "Not really. I just heard that he got drunk and drove into the river. Is there more?"

I nodded. I was just about to tell her about Daniel when Mama called up the stairs. "River, I need you girls to help me."

I stood up. "We have to get out of this room," I say to Meadow Lark.

But she kept sitting on Theron's bed. "Didn't anyone, like your mom and dad, go look for him?"

"He told them not to, so they didn't. Theron just turned eighteen, and Daddy say eighteen is an adult and you have to take responsibility for your own actions. And he say that if Theron ever did come back, there could be trouble with the law."

"Well, what about the police—didn't any police come for him?"

I shook my head. "They come next morning, but Theron was gone by then. So Daddy wasn't lying when he say he didn't know where Theron was. And now they just don't talk about him."

I didn't tell her that Mama cried for two weeks and stopped humming in the kitchen after Theron left us.

Finally, Meadow Lark got off the bed, as if she'd heard all the story she wanted. "Maybe they don't talk about him. But they haven't forgotten him. I'm sure of that," she say.

Like me, I thought. *I would never forget him.*

As we tiptoed out to the hall, she turned around and say, "I have to tell you something very important. I walk in my sleep. If you see me do that, you can't wake me up."

"What happens if I wake you up?" I asked.

"There's no telling. So if I sleepwalk, just put me back in bed."

I nodded. "And don't wake you up."

"So, can I still stay here?"

"Why not?"

"Because it's a strange thing to do."

It wasn't strange—it was another interesting thing about Meadow Lark, along with her eye and her leg and that she come from Arizona and was in the hospital four times.

As Meadow Lark went downstairs, I smoothed out the comforter where she had sat. Then I took one more look at the room to make sure nothing was out of place, that nothing was moved and nothing was different. Because I knew that changing Theron's room would change Theron. And that would change us.

Chapter 8

Daniel Bunch was not in art class on Monday, and he wasn't in the quad at lunch on Tuesday to pester me. By Wednesday, the worry that had settled in me as I watched our wish slide down the river sat up and looked around.

"Where's Daniel?" Sonya asked to the middle of the art table.

When class began, Ms. Zucchero had put a pile of things on the table—a CrimsonCrisp apple with a brown bite in it, a tube of Colgate rolled up halfway, a Slinky with kinks in it, a picture of a brown-haired girl who looked a lot like Ms. Zucchero, a paperback book with the cover half torn off, and one of Ms. Zucchero's crocheted squares with a hook stuck through it.

"I liked your collages so much that I brought my own collection," she say. "These are just some of the things I found in my car yesterday."

Then she told us to draw what we saw without looking at our sketch pads — just let our pencils move across the shapes in our minds. So everyone was not looking at their sketch pads and not looking at one another, but talking to the pile in the middle of the table.

On the other side of the pile was where Daniel Bunch would be sitting if he were in school, and the gap he left was like when a tooth falls out. I kept wiggling that space with my eyes, to make sure he truly wasn't in it. Because even if Daniel Bunch was absent, in my mind he sat there just like always, watching me and waiting to pounce.

"Daisy Crumb said he's sick," Kevin Kale say to the pile. "He has a hundred and four fever."

"What's that mean?" Sonya asked.

All the water left my mouth, and my hand holding the pencil shook so to hear about Daniel Bunch being sick. I looked down at my sketch pad, and I had just drawn something that looked like a clump of hair in the bathtub drain. And the worry in my heart nodded at me and say, *Isn't that what you asked for?*

Even before Kevin answered, I knew it was bad. Theron once had a 103 fever, and Mama put him in the tub with ice water until he cooled down. Even when he called to me, I wouldn't go into the bathroom to see him. I thought if I didn't see him, I wouldn't miss him as much after he died from that fever.

Kevin answered Sonya in the same voice he announced what page we were on. "Your brain can melt when you have a fever that high."

"Which can only happen to people who have a brain," Martin say. "So Bunch is safe."

I wondered what Daniel would think if he knew how they talked about him when he wasn't there.

"Oh no," Sonya say.

All during those three days he'd been absent, no one seemed to notice or care what had happened to Daniel Bunch. And now, no one seemed scared except me. I was the only person in the room who had wished that Daniel Bunch would disappear and then floated the wish down the river.

"Focus, people," Ms. Zucchero say from her desk, "or we'll have quiet time."

Everyone knew that meant no talking until the bell rang. Usually we listened to Ms. Zucchero when she had quiet time. I wished she had made quiet time before Daniel Bunch trashed my collage last Friday.

Martin slid his sketch pad across the table and stretched out his arms. "Anyway, he's at the hospital."

Now my sketch pad trembled so bad in my hand that I let go of it, and it clapped to the floor. When I bent to pick it up, I had to swallow hard to keep from gagging.

"How do you know *that*?" Sonya asked, tossing her ponytail. "Did you see him go?"

When Martin didn't answer, she asked again, "Did you see him?" This time her voice sounded like it was flapping on a clothesline.

Fear slapped my chest and dribbled into every cell of my body. I stared at the picture of the brown-haired girl and tried to draw the smooth line down her cheek, but I felt my hand making a long squiggle on the page. If Daniel Bunch got sick before Meadow Lark and I made the wish on Friday afternoon, then we had nothing to do with Daniel's 104 fever and his being in the hospital. But if he got sick after we made the wish, then it might have been our fault.

I swallowed again, and without thinking I asked, "When did they take him to the hospital?"

"She talks," Kevin whispered.

Just then Ms. Zucchero shifted in her chair. It was her signal for what was to come. "Okay, people. Quiet time now."

Then Sonya say, "The fake-accent girl talks. Why would she care what happened to Daniel?"

She was a fly in my ear, and I waved her away and asked again. "Does anyone know when they take him?"

But Sonya just kept talking to the pile. "Maybe she likes him. Or maybe she knows more than she's telling. You gotta watch out for the quiet ones, because they're always listening. Maybe if we listen, we'll find out what she knows. Talk, fake-accent girl."

My heart pounded, and I couldn't catch my breath. "Anyone know?" I asked, looking at Martin.

"Quiet, people," Ms. Zucchero say to our table.

When she looked back at her crocheting, Martin whispered, "They took him on Sunday."

Sonya must really like Daniel, I thought, because she blushed deeper than that CrimsonCrisp in the middle of the table and say, "No, Martin, you're a liar."

The next thing I remembered was feeling dizzy like when you get to the bottom of a roller coaster, and hearing a knock on the floor—which I later realized was my head—and then Ms. Zucchero looking down at me.

"River, can you sit up?" she asked, squeezing my arm. My head was buzzing. "We need to take you to Mrs. Bertetti's office. Someone bring her some water."

Then Ms. Zucchero wheeled her chair over to me and helped me sit in it. I cried a little because she was being so careful with me and because everyone stared and say how pale I looked. Ms. Zucchero couldn't have wheeled me out fast enough.

She rolled me down to Mrs. Bertetti, the school nurse. The two of them talked and Mrs. Bertetti told me to lie down on the bed with my knees up.

"I hope you feel better soon," Ms. Zucchero say before she left to go back to class.

Mrs. Bertetti took my temperature, which was normal, and then held my wrist with her fingertips while she looked at her watch. Her lips moved as she stared at it.

Finally she put my hand back down on the bed and asked, "Can your mother drive you home?"

I shook my head. "She doesn't drive. She stopped driving . . . a while ago." Mrs. Bertetti didn't have to know everything. "But I can walk home."

"Not after that tumble. What about your father?"

"He's in New York." Daddy had left again almost as soon as he'd come back from Orlando.

"Your brother? Oh—" Mrs. Bertetti say, cutting herself off.

Everything today reminded me of Theron. I just wanted to go home.

Maybe she felt bad for bringing up Theron, so she went out of the nurse's office for a few minutes and come back with a glass of water and set it on the table beside me. "I called your mother. She'll find you a ride home."

As she took my pulse again, I looked up at the ceiling tiles and asked, "Do you know Daniel Bunch?"

"I know all my students," she say, and set my hand back down beside me. "Is Daniel your friend?"

"He's in my art class."

"Then you must know he's sick."

I was glad to be lying down, or I'd have probably fainted again. But I had to find out as much as I could. "Is he in the hospital?"

"Because he's your friend, I'll tell you that he is in the hospital. But I don't know anything more."

Then Mrs. Bertetti sat down at her desk and started writing on a form. "What did you eat for breakfast?" she asked.

I sat up, propping myself on my elbows. "When did Daniel go to the hospital?"

She didn't take her eyes off her desk when she told me, almost in a whisper, "I heard it was Sunday. Now that's it. No more information, okay?"

"Oh," I say, and my heart pounded so strong that I thought it would fling me off the bed. I sank back down onto the mattress. And then the worry nodded at me and say, *Wishes are powerful things.*

Mrs. Bertetti stopped writing and looked up. "I'm sure it would make him very happy if you paid him a visit."

Chapter 9

"It was just a coincidence," I say to Meadow Lark. "Nothing more than that."

Meadow Lark was sitting W on her bed, and I was trying to sit crisscross, but it hurt the insides of my knees. I liked that she and I shared the way we sat and that, for a while at least, we shared the same room. It was like we were friends, almost like sisters.

She had set Mr. Tricks's cage on her bed and was making kissing noises at him. Mr. Tricks strutted headfirst over to the wires and blinked at her. "That was more than a coincidence, and you know it," she say.

I slid the facecloth off my forehead and tossed it on the night table, next to the glass of ginger ale Mama had brought to me. When she first laid that cool facecloth across my forehead, it felt so good. But soon it turned warm and dirty-feeling, like a tea bag on a saucer.

"We make a wish, and then Daniel Bunch goes to the hospital," she say, and kiss-kissed close to the cage. "That's not how coincidences work, is it, Mr. Tricks?"

"They happen all the time like that. You hear a word you've never heard before and the next thing you know, you hear it fifteen times. A song come into your head, and then the next person you see is singing it. Those are coincidences, just like Daniel Bunch just happened to get sick after we just happened to make a wish about it."

"Things like that happen to you?" she asked.

"Don't they happen to everyone?"

"Not me. But that was no coincidence," she say, and opened the paper lunch bag that Mama put together for her that morning. She pulled out a zipper bag of carrot sticks. "Want some?"

I shook my head and closed my eyes. The Cheetos I ate at lunch now sat on my stomach like a brick. They tasted good when I ate them, but that was before I heard about Daniel Bunch.

Meadow Lark kept harping. "Was it a coincidence we were put in the same homeroom?" she asked. "Or another coincidence that we went to the river at the same time? Or that we found Mr. Tricks just when he needed us?"

"I think so," I say, though she had a point. "What do *you* call them?"

"I don't know," Meadow Lark say, "except not coincidences." She bit off some carrot and chewed it. "I call them miracles."

"You and Mama should talk."

Mr. Tricks cocked his head at one angle and then another, as Meadow Lark spoke.

"He *can't* be sick just because we wished it," I say.

"Are you scared that maybe he is, and it's true?" she mumbled.

Then she spit the chewed-up carrot onto her finger and stuck it between the wires of the cage. Mr. Tricks stretched his neck and pecked the carrot off her finger, then opened his beak and shook his head at her like he expected more. Mr. Tricks was in love with Meadow Lark.

"I'm scared," she say, answering her own question.

"Me too," I say. "I just don't want to believe we made him sick."

Then Meadow Lark turned the lunch bag upside down and shook out a napkin, the same kind of napkin Mama put in my bag that morning. But in the corner of Meadow Lark's napkin was a little red heart, just like the one I saw the first day we met.

"Look, we don't even know for sure he's sick,"

Meadow Lark say, wiping her fingers on that napkin with the heart drawn on it. "Kids exaggerate all the time." Then she popped the rest of the carrot in her mouth. "Especially those kids."

"But Mrs. Bertetti even say it was true." I tried to hide that my lip quivered and my voice flapped just like Sonya's when she heard that Daniel Bunch was in the hospital. Meadow Lark's napkin had a red heart on it and mine did not. I never had a red heart on a napkin.

Meadow Lark spit more carrot onto her finger and swallowed the rest. "It could just be a rumor and she heard it and believed it and told it to you." Then she folded up the napkin into quarters, with the heart on the outside.

I had something that was better than a red heart. I got up and opened my ballerina box and took out the little emerald ring and pressed it into the top of my thumb like a crown, and held it out to Meadow Lark. "See my ring?"

Meadow Lark finished feeding the carrot to Mr. Tricks. "Pretty. Where did you get it?"

"In the river . . . I think. It's my favorite thing." Then I took off the ring and set it down. My head still hurt, and I lay back down on my bed.

"So, back to Daniel," she say. "We have to find

out if the rumor is true," Meadow Lark say, as if I had interrupted her by showing her the ring. "One of us has to go to the hospital to make sure, or we'll just wonder about it the rest of our lives. We can't be scared forever." She popped the last carrot in her mouth and put Mr. Tricks's cage back on the floor.

My stomach gurgled and I rolled onto my side to face her. "What if he *is* there? What if he *is* sick? Then what do we do?"

"I don't know—we'll figure something out. Nothing like this ever happened to me before, so we'll take it one step at a time."

"But you're the one who wrote the wish. I thought you knew all about wishes. And then you put it in the river. I thought you knew what you were doing."

"Well, one of us has to go to the hospital," she say, "and it won't be me. I've had enough of hospitals for a long time."

I knew she would be as stubborn about not going to the hospital as I was about not going into the water, so to save time I sat up and finished the ginger ale all at once, and then I worked out a burp that sounded like "I'll go." That's how we decided.

The fact was, I knew from the start it would be me. Unless I saw Daniel Bunch in the hospital with my own eyes, I wouldn't believe he was sick. Even if Meadow Lark went and come back and told me it was true, I'd still want to see for myself.

"I just have to figure out how. And with Mama around, we will need a miracle."

Meadow Lark got up and crumpled the lunch bag and tossed it in the wastebasket. But I noticed she saved the napkin and slipped it into her bureau drawer.

"Mr. Tricks must hate being in that cage after being out in the wild all his life," she say, opening the cage. Mr. Tricks looked at the open door and strutted right out like he owned the place.

"Okay," I say, "but don't forget to put him back in and shut the door tight."

Even though Meadow Lark warned me about her sleepwalking, she caught me off guard that night. Mr. Tricks cooed and woke me up, and when I got up to see what was wrong with him, I noticed that Meadow Lark wasn't in her bed.

"Meadow Lark?" I whispered, but she didn't answer.

Our door was open, so I stepped out. Meadow Lark was walking down the hall toward Theron's room. She stopped at the door and put her hand on the knob.

"Meadow Lark," I say again, careful not to wake her up.

She must have heard me that time, because she turned around and, without looking at me, walked back to the room and got into her bed.

That was it, but I lay awake for a long time after that to make sure she didn't get up again.

Without realizing it, Mama helped me see Daniel the next day.

"Does your head still hurt, dear?" she asked as I lay in bed with the comforter up to my nose. Her hand on my forehead felt as cool as that facecloth did.

"Now it's my stomach," I groaned.

Meadow Lark, all ready for school with her backpack over her shoulder and her lunch bag in her hand, stood a few feet behind Mama. For a second I wondered if she had another red heart on her napkin in that lunch bag.

Mama sat back. "I have to work extra hours today, which means I'll be gone until near suppertime. I could call in sick so I can stay home with you," she say, but I knew she wanted those extra hours.

"You can't miss work, Mama," I say, trying to make my voice crackle. "Besides, I'm old enough to stay home by myself now." After all, according to Mr. Clapton, I was almost in high school.

"I'll tell school you're sick today," Meadow Lark say, and widened her good eye as if she were telling me, *This is your miracle!* Meadow Lark seemed to have recovered from her episode the night before.

"Yes, you are," Mama say, and smoothed out my comforter. "I sure hope you feel better by tonight. Daddy's coming home, and I'm making a roast."

Chapter 10

I hadn't ridden my bike since last fall. It hung in the garage next to Theron's Giant. Theron had mowed lawns, shoveled snow, helped Sonya's daddy paint houses, and tutored for an entire year for the money to buy his bike, and it was his treasure. How I wanted to ride it to the hospital, grip the same handlebars my brother gripped and slice through the wind just like he did. But Theron had a rule that only he could touch that bike he worked so hard to buy. And now, just like my bike from the Goodwill, his treasure was shrouded in dust and cobwebs.

After carefully unhooking my bike and wiping it down, I set off for the hospital, riding low so that no one would see me and ask why I wasn't in school. Or worse, tell Mama.

"Bunch, Daniel," say the nurse, a man with big pores and hair that stuck out like a brush, to his computer screen. "Room three-fourteen."

It was only when I asked, "Which way is three-fourteen?" that he looked up at me.

His eye narrowed. "How old are you?"

"Twelve." I added a year, because in some places that year made a difference between being allowed or forbidden to visit.

"You can't visit without an adult," he say. "Where is your adult?"

"My mama's parking the car," I say, which was a lie in every universe. "She told me to hurry and see Daniel before visiting hours were over."

"Your mama does know that visiting hours don't end until eight, doesn't she?"

To stop myself from telling any more lies, like the one about Mama only understanding Portuguese and the one about us being from Alaska, I just stood there. He looked at me hard. I thought he was going to send me home, but then he pointed to the left. "Go on," he say, "Three-fourteen's down that way, end of the hall. You're his first visitor."

"Today?"

"Ever. I'll send your mama there . . . after she parks the car."

My legs felt like noodles and my pulse played drums in my ears as I walked down the hall toward Daniel's room. It was my own fault I was here. I might not believe that Daniel was in the hospital because of Meadow Lark and me, but she did, and it was my duty as her friend to see how bad off he actually was. So I kept walking toward room 314 and wishing I wasn't so scared.

Daniel Bunch's door was open a crack, and I stood outside, breathing slowly and trying to stop shaking, not knowing what I'd see. I actually hoped Daniel would be nasty to me, like he usually was, because that would mean he wasn't sick. It would mean everyone was wrong.

"Hello," come a voice from across the hall.

"Hello," I say. I couldn't see anyone, so I walked toward the voice and looked in the room. "Do you need something—a nurse?"

A boy with a mop of sandy-colored hair half sat up in the hospital bed reading an Edgar Allan Poe comic book. A cast covering his whole leg hung just above the bed, aimed at the TV on the wall.

"Password," the boy say, and lay his comic book down on his stomach.

"Hmm," I say, and looked at the title. "Usher."

His face grew a smile. "Impressive." The boy's teeth were so short that it looked like he didn't have any, and his cheeks were patchy red, like they'd been rubbed with snowballs.

"Either you're a genius or a mind reader," he say. "Or perhaps the password is too obvious. I'll have to change it as a precaution."

"You could have just say I was wrong."

"I could have," he say, "but that would have been dishonest." Then he took in a breath. "Are you here to visit someone? That boy across the hall, perhaps?"

I nodded. "The nurse say that's Daniel Bunch's room."

"It is his room. Are you his . . . sister, a friend, a . . . ?"

"I go to school with him."

"Oh. Has anyone ever told you that you have an unusual way of talking?"

Him too? I thought. "Yes, everyone say that."

He crossed his arms. "And I'm sure you get teased about it."

I shrugged. "I can't help it," I say. "I woke up one morning after my brother leave us and I start talking like this." Then I glanced across the hall for a glimpse of Daniel. A glimpse was all I wanted of him at the moment. And then maybe another glimpse, and then I would have the courage to see him.

The boy scratched his chin and looked at the ceiling. "I've read about that. It's rare, but it has a name. People wake up talking with a French accent or an Australian accent or a Japanese accent. You found your accent somewhere very far south of New Hampshire — I'd say from somewhere in the Carolinas."

"Well, I wasn't looking for it, so it must have found me."

"That's an interesting way of describing it," he say, and picked up his comic book. "Just so you know, it's rather charming. However, if you don't like it, you can force yourself to lose it."

"You talk funny too," I told him. "You sound like a professor."

When he finished ha-ha-ha-ing behind his comic book, he say, "Actually, you *are* a mind reader, because that's what I'm called — Professor — by people who don't understand me. My real name is Benjamin," he added with a little bow of his head.

"I'm River," I say, and bow back at him.

"Pleasure meeting you," he say. "By the way, if you're here to see Daniel Bunch, you'll have to do all the talking, because he's extremely ill."

"Oh," I say, suddenly agitated at the mention of Daniel, and I hoped Benjamin wouldn't see my heart beating through my T-shirt.

"Sorry if that upset you," he say.

"It's just a big shock. Is he really that sick?"

"He might even be dead, but go see for yourself."

So what everyone in art class say was true. And maybe what Meadow Lark say was true too—that it wasn't a coincidence, and it was our fault Daniel was in the hospital.

I looked at Benjamin. "It's time. I have to see him now."

This wasn't like when Theron had his 103-degree fever in the bathtub and I had the choice not to look. This was different. When Benjamin say Daniel was so sick, I began to believe that it was our fault, so I had to pay him a visit and report back to Meadow Lark.

"It was a pleasure meeting you," Benjamin say with another little bow, and I wandered out of his room and across the hall.

I knocked lightly on the door, and when there was no answer, I pushed it open and stepped inside.

The room smelled like rubbing alcohol and bleach. Daniel lay flat in the hospital bed with his eyes closed, as still as a corpse, and white as the pillowcase under his head. His left arm, now in a support bandage, rested on a rolled-up towel at his side.

Out of respect for his state of possible death, I drew the curtain closed around his bed. Then I stared at him for a minute or so, watching for a telltale eyebrow twitch and listening for a sigh or a stomach gurgle.

"Is he alive?" Benjamin asked from across the hall.

I waved my hand in front of Daniel's eyes, but he didn't move. "I'll find out," I whispered, loud enough to carry.

Daddy once told me that when he and Mama first brought me home, I slept so quiet and still that they were terrified I'd stopped breathing in my sleep. So Daddy would hold a little mirror under my nose. If he saw vapor on the mirror, he knew I was still alive. Remembering that, I looked around Daniel's room for something to put under his nose.

A butter knife lay on a tray near the window. I grabbed it and turned back to Daniel. But just as I was about to slide the knife under his nose, the curtain rings screeched, and the nurse from the front desk stood there with his hands on his hips.

"Your mother must've gotten lost in the parking lot. Time to go," he say. And then he saw the butter knife. "Hey, what's that?"

At exactly that moment, Daniel come out of his coma, and saw the knife.

"She's trying to kill me!" he screamed, sitting full up in bed. "She tried to slice me open!" Then, *"Oww!"*

he shrieked, and clutched his throat, as if that dull little knife had actually touched him.

I ran out of the room, down the hall, down the stairs, and out the revolving door. Then I tossed the butter knife into some bushes, hopped on my bike, and took off.

Pedaling home as fast as I could, I felt glad about one thing—if Daniel Bunch was dying, it was certain he wouldn't die that day. Because when he sat up and saw that knife in my hand and screamed at me like that, he looked like the same Daniel Bunch that told me in art class that my collage stunk.

If what Meadow Lark say was true—that we made Daniel Bunch sick by wishing it—then we had to make another wish to make him well again. And we would have to do it fast, before he got any sicker. We would go have to go down to the river and float a get-well wish for Daniel Bunch. Meadow Lark would be home from school when I got home, and Mama would still be at work. So if we hurried, Mama would never know we were gone.

When I got home, I carefully hung my bike back on its hook next to Theron's and went into the house, expecting to see Meadow Lark on the sofa or in the kitchen. But the house was quiet.

"Meadow Lark?" I called, and when she didn't

answer, I went upstairs to our room. "Meadow Lark?" I say again as I pushed open the door.

She lay on the bed, rolled up with her back to me and shaking so hard that the bed jiggled.

"What's so funny?" I asked.

She turned over to face me, and when I saw her two puffy, red eyes, I knew different. Meadow Lark was crying.

"He's gone," she say, and wiped her nose with the back of her hand.

"Who's . . . gone?" I asked, and then a horror pierced my heart. "You mean Daniel Bunch?" Did she hear something after I left the hospital?

Meadow Lark shook her head and pointed to Mr. Tricks's cage on the floor—his empty cage— and then to the window. It was open just enough for a pigeon the size of Mr. Tricks to strut through and fly away.

Chapter 11

Meadow Lark sniffled all the way to the river, and every once in a while along the way, as if she saw the empty cage for the first time all over again, she say things like "Mr. Tricks flew out the window!" and "Our poor pidge! His wing wasn't even healed."

"Maybe we didn't look hard enough," I say. "Maybe he's stuck somewhere in the room—did you look behind the bureau, under the beds—"

"I looked everywhere, River. We looked everywhere. There's only one place he went, and that was out the window. He probably fell because he can't fly, and then got eaten up . . . or worse."

"Is there anything worse?" I asked.

"Torture is worse."

"Maybe he'll come back here. Maybe he's a homing pigeon, and don't homing pigeons go back to where they come from?"

"You sound like you don't even care about him," Meadow Lark say, and sniffled. "You haven't even cried for him."

By then we'd reached the beach, and I say, "Of course I care about Mr. Tricks. I care if he fell out or got eaten or tortured. But—I'm sorry, Meadow Lark—right now, undoing the wish about Daniel Bunch is more important."

The truth was, I feared there was nothing left of Mr. Tricks but a little skeleton and a couple white feathers, though I kept that to myself.

"Let's hurry up, then, so we can find our bird," she say.

Meadow Lark and I sat on the rock, and she pulled a pen and some paper out of her pocket.

"You'll have to write. I just can't now," she say, and then her face twisted up and she cried some more for Mr. Tricks.

I took the pen from her. "I'll do it," I say, partly because I knew she was too sad and partly because I didn't want the wish for Daniel to get crossed out or erased this time. It had to be perfect when we sent it off. "I'll write them both."

I clicked the pen and wrote, *We wish Daniel Bunch to get better soon*, and then showed it to Meadow Lark. "How's this?"

"Be more specific," she say quietly, and wiped her nose with the back of her hand. "We might not have another chance."

Who was being persnickety now? I thought, but I say, "You're right," just because she was so distressed.

She gave me a new piece of paper, and this time I wrote: *We wish Daniel Bunch to get completely and wholly healthy immediately and right away.*

"That's good. Now, it's Mr. Tricks's turn," she say, and gave me a new piece of paper.

I touched the pen to my lips and thought about what to write, specifically, and then wrote: *We wish Mr. Tricks to come back.*

"Alive," she say, peering at the paper.

Alive, I wrote.

"And not hurt."

And not hurt, I wrote, and then, just to be sure, added: *Perfectly fine.*

She nodded, her face still puffy from crying. "That's good. Now we'll send them off. You do it this time," she say, but I pushed the wishes at her.

"You have to—you know that."

"And you have to get over that," she say, shaking her head so her hair shivered around her shoulders. "It's just water."

"I've tried. I want to, but I can't."

"I just don't understand . . . how can you be afraid of the water but want to come here?"

"I don't know," I say. "It's just like a magic place here." As I say that, I realized it had gotten even more magical since I met Meadow Lark.

"Maybe," she say, and slid off the rock and grabbed my hand. "We'll go out there together."

But I yanked my hand out of hers. "No! I just can't," I say, and watched the river race by.

"Oh, all right," she say, and stepped into the water. "But one day you will."

She walked out up to her calves, to where the current ran strong. Then she held up the pieces of paper to show them to me and called, "Here they go," and dropped them into the water. Right away the river grabbed those wishes and whisked them off. I watched them slip downriver until they disappeared into the ripples.

As I sat on the rock and watched Meadow Lark, all around me the river roared and gurgled and murmured like a thousand voices, all blending into one, saying, *Don't worry*, like a whisper up behind me.

"They're gone," Meadow Lark called. "We can stop worrying now."

Whether it was a coincidence or not that both spoke the same words at the same time, that same chill ran up to my scalp, and I shivered.

"We've done everything we can," she say. Then she pointed downriver. "Hey, what's that bridge down there? I've never seen that."

"We're not supposed to go there, remember?"

"Why not? It looks interesting."

"It's old . . . and scary, and everyone stays off it."

She stepped out of the water and put her sandals back on. I thought her curiosity about the bridge was over, but then she say, "So let's go walk on it."

"No, it's dangerous. It's off-limits."

"Who said?"

"Everyone—Mama and Daddy, everyone."

She acted like she hadn't heard me, and started walking toward the end of the beach where it met the woods. "Come on, River. We might find Mr. Tricks there."

I couldn't stop her, and I didn't want her to get lost, so I followed her into the woods. Even with her slow leg, she'd gotten far ahead of me fast.

"Wait!" I called, trying to keep up with her through the thick underbrush of the forest.

A few yards later she stopped suddenly and

whirled around and tugged at her shirt.

"Help me, River!" she called. "I'm stuck."

A branch had snared her shirt, and the harder she tried to untangle it, the higher it slid up her body. It was only for an instant, but long enough for me to see a map of scars on her belly. Then she tore her shirt free and stuffed the hem into her shorts. As she did, I pretended to study a perfect fern.

"You okay?" I asked.

She slid her hair behind her ears and nodded, her hair bouncing. "That's what it feels like to be trapped," she say. "That's how Mr. Tricks felt when we found him."

"We should go back," I say, looking behind me. I could hardly see the beach now beyond the canopy of green and shade and brush, which softened the roar of the river into a steady hush.

"What's over here?" she asked, and headed toward the riverbank.

"Just the river. Come on, Meadow Lark. Let's go back and look for Mr. Tricks."

"I want to see," she say, and took off. I followed her a few more yards, and then the woods opened to a little cove sheltered by oaks and aspen trees sweeping the surface of the water.

"River . . . what's that?" she asked, pointing toward the cove at a log, half covered with mud and leaves and vines, jutting out from the bank. At the very end of it was a big, round burl that looked something like a head.

Meadow Lark stepped over to it.

"Be careful with your leg," I say, close behind.

We squatted as close as we could without falling into the water, and then Meadow Lark leaned over and ran her hands over the bark.

"It has something stuck to it," she say, and handed me a square of paper.

Seeing that paper come off the log grabbed my breath. It was lined paper, just like the kind we wrote our wishes on. I knew before I unfolded it that I would see Meadow Lark's handwriting on it. And I knew she would find another square of paper with my writing on it. I also knew that if we looked long enough on that log, we'd find the white feather we made our first wish on.

Meadow Lark started scraping away the mud from the log, and together we cleared away the leaves and vines. Then we saw that the log didn't just seem to have a head, but the way the branches grew out from each side looked like —

"They look like wings," Meadow Lark say.

"Like wings," I echoed, hearing the flutter in my voice.

Meadow Lark held her hand to her throat. "River, do you know what this is? We found ourselves an angel."

Chapter 12

Meadow Lark stared and shook her head at that log. "I can't believe it—an angel, right here at our river."

"Stop being so dramatic, Meadow Lark. It's just a log, can't you see?" I say, and blinked away any doubt. It wasn't an angel. Angels had white robes and white wings. They sang and flew around and brought messages and untangled people from their troubles. This wasn't an angel—this was a log.

"Even with one good eye I can see it," she say, tossing her hair behind her shoulders. "It has wings. And it has a head."

Rain began to fall, tapping the trees above and around us. I blinked again. "No, that's just a giant burl with moss growing on it."

"Then how do you explain those?" she asked, pointing to the bits of paper stuck to the log.

"The current carried them," I say, watching the way the water curled into the little cove and then swirled in front of the log, teasing it. "Just like it carries everything."

Meadow Lark put her finger on her chin and sat, sticking her slow leg out in front of her. "I think the current was taking them to where they needed to go—and this was the place."

I felt disappointed that the wishes we floated down the river ended up on a log, which wasn't special or magical—it was just a log that caught trash. And I was disappointed in Meadow Lark for putting the idea in my head that our wishes could come true, and betrayed by the river for not taking the wishes far away.

"I think we should take them off and let them go again," I say.

"No! They're here for a reason. I don't know what, but they need to stay here."

"Meadow Lark," I say, stepping closer to her, "there's such a thing as looking too hard for things that aren't there."

"You're so sure about that," she say, as she studied the log. "Well, just in case, we need to hide this angel so no one else finds it. No telling what they'd do to it."

"You mean, like Daniel Bunch?" I say. "He isn't smart enough to find this. Daniel only finds rusty nails and gum wrappers, because they're all he expects to find."

"You're right . . . he has no imagination," she say. "If he saw this, he'd think it was just a log."

I sat down beside her. "Are you trying to make a point?"

The rain had let up, and the leaves appeared translucent. A sparrow called and slid over the smooth surface of the water, and the smell of pine needles filled the air.

I stared at that log so long that everything around it disappeared, and gradually something like a face began to emerge on that burl. I looked away from the face and shook my head.

"No, I don't believe in any of that. Hoping for things to happen—for people to get sick or get better, or to go away or come back—is a waste of time and it just makes you sad when those things don't happen."

I glanced at the log again, and blinked away what began to look like a nose.

"It's good to have something to hope for," Meadow Lark say. "Life would be so dull and boring and sad if you didn't."

"But what if it never happens?"

"Well," she say, touching the log, "you keep hoping.

As long as it doesn't happen, you always have something to hope for."

"Mama hopes. I think that's how she can stand it that Theron's gone." I twisted off a piece of vine and tossed it on the water. "What do you hope for?" I asked, watching the vine drift away.

Meadow Lark leaned back on her hands and looked up at the sky for a long time. Finally she say, "A really nice bed, something good to eat every night, the same teacher for a whole school year . . . a best friend, and Mr. Tricks."

The sparrow had stopped calling, and a shadow moved above us. Raindrops tapped on the leaves and blurred the water.

I stared at the log and tried not to see a face in it. "Well, it's still just a log."

"People make fun of my eye," she say, "but I can see better than some of them can."

The wind stirred the trees above us, and a whisper passed by me. Just when I thought I knew Meadow Lark, she become a mystery again. Maybe, I thought, if she had that kind of sight, she could help me understand something about that house, so I took a breath and say, "Sometimes I see a house that I've never been to before, but it's so familiar to me."

Instead of laughing at me or looking surprised, Meadow Lark leaned forward. "Is this house in a dream?" she asked.

"Not really. It always happens when I'm awake."

"Do you know everything about the house? Are people in the house?"

"No, it makes more of itself the farther I go into it. I can't explain, except it only exists a few feet around me at a time. And there's never anyone in the house—I always feel like I'm the only one there."

"Wow," she say. "What do you think it's all about?"

"I don't know. But I feel . . . like there's something in there for me. I just have to wait and find it."

"It's like the house wants to show you something. *Ooh*," she say, and rubbed her arms. "I've got goose bumps. Next time, try to stay longer and see what happens."

I shivered and rubbed my goose bumps too. "I'll try. I just wish I knew what it all means."

"I wish I could do that—go to a house like that."

"I wish I could stop."

"We have so many wishes but no more paper."

"We don't need paper, Meadow Lark—we have *a log*."

"An angel," she say, and stretched her arms above her head. It made her shirt ride up again, and in the

gap above her shorts I saw the scars again. Sympathy
pains chafed the back of my calves. "Why do you
have those?" I asked.

Meadow Lark yanked her shirt all the way over
her belly, and I knew her scars embarrassed her.
"When I was born, my insides were upside down.
It's called *situs inversus* — but that's what it means. I've
had a lot of operations."

As she talked, I noticed that she ran a finger lightly
over her shirt. Meadow Lark didn't need to see the
scars to know where they were. She probably spent
a lot of time tracing them when she was alone, and
by now she knew every one of them, the same way I
knew each thing I'd found in the river and every item
in Theron's room.

"They had to put everything where it belonged."

"Is that why you were in the hospital so many
times?"

She nodded, making the pine needles under her
head crackle. "They say I'll always have the scars,
even though they'll fade after a while."

Then Meadow Lark scooped a handful of pine
needles. "I really wish Mr. Tricks would come back."

"Me too," I say. "I don't want to lose another
thing. But we need to do more than wish for him."

"Then we have to keep looking until we find

him." Meadow Lark sighed and tossed her handful of pine needles into the air. They landed in her hair and settled back on the ground.

"Also," I say, "we have to look for him because . . . if we don't, he won't know we missed him. He won't know we wanted him."

Meadow Lark looked solemn, like the day she walked into art class with the carnations for Ms. Zucchero. "We could start by asking your mom if she knows where he is."

"Why ask my mama?"

Then, real slowly, Meadow Lark say, "Well, didn't you say she . . . doesn't like birds?"

"No, she doesn't." Then I understood what she meant, and I didn't like it. "You think Mama let Mr. Tricks out?"

Meadow Lark turned to me with her one big, open eye and nodded. "It makes sense, doesn't it?"

"No, it doesn't, and I can't believe you would say that. I can't believe you would think that. Mr. Tricks, he got himself out."

"Well, you asked, River, and that's what I was thinking."

"Well, you were thinking wrong!" I cried. I sprang up and ran out of the woods, leaving Meadow Lark behind. I stumbled through the underbrush, then ran across the beach and up the path to the library.

"Keep your stupid log!" I shouted behind me. But all the time I was running away from Meadow Lark and what she say about Mama, my pulse thumped my ears to the rhythm of the words in my head: *Mama let him out. Mama let him out.*

I knew Meadow Lark was following me, but even though she couldn't keep up with me — or *because* she couldn't — I just ran faster and harder, until I could no longer hear her voice calling me to wait.

Chapter 13

The screen door shuddered close behind me, and the aroma of Mama's pot roast and potatoes filled my nose. It almost made me forget what had just happened between Meadow Lark and me, because those smells meant Daddy was home.

"Forgive and be free" was one of those things Mama often told me, so as those dinner smells poked the sides of my throat, I made up my mind to consider forgiving Meadow Lark. Though I might be able to forgive her, I couldn't forget, because that chant still flowed in my veins—*Mama let him out*—and because it was Meadow Lark who had put it there.

"Daddy?" I called as I followed the yummy smells. I found him in the kitchen, slicing pot roast with a long knife and wearing his chef's apron that say MINNESOTA: L'ÉTOILE DU NORD.

I ran and put my arms around him, and he hugged me back the best he could with a knife in his hand.

"I missed you," he say.

"River Rose Byrne," Mama called from the dining room, "you recovered awfully fast."

"Oh," I say, and glanced at Daddy. "I think it was
a six-hour thing."

Mama come into the kitchen and put her hands
on her hips, and looked at me long and hard. Then
her face softened. "I'm glad you're feeling better," she
say, "but I can smell where you've been. And what
have we told you over and over about going there?"

"Well, it can't smell as good as what you're making for supper."

"I didn't say you smelled *good*," Mama say back,
but her voice had an almost smile to it. "Go upstairs
and wash it off. You and your friend."

"Meadow Lark—" *Isn't my friend*, I wanted to say.
"She'll be here soon."

Mama pulled down one of her good serving bowls
with the gold rim from the cupboard over the stove.
"You mean to say you left her there, with that slow
leg of hers?"

"No . . . yes," I say, as guilt took hold of me. I did
leave her there, when she couldn't run very fast. "I'll
go get her if she doesn't come back soon."

We waited twenty minutes for Meadow Lark,
and Mama put the food in the oven to keep warm.

Just as I was about to go back to get her, Meadow Lark opened the screen door. She smiled at me and say, "Everyone's home now? Good. I'm starving," and went upstairs.

When I got up to our room, she was rubbing the river off her with a facecloth.

"What took you so long?" I asked.

"I went down to that old broken-down bridge—"

"You have to stay off that bridge. It's the one that—"

"I know, the one that got flooded a long time ago. Your family has so many rules. 'Don't go there.' 'Stay out of that bedroom.' 'Sit out here after supper.' You've had your whole life to learn them all, but I've had only a few days."

"If Mama finds out what you did . . ."

"You're the only one that told me to stay away from that bridge, so I went on it. And see? It didn't collapse. I didn't fall in."

Meadow Lark seemed to have forgotten that I abandoned her at the river, because she wasn't acting mad at me. When someone isn't mad at you the way you expect them to be, being mad at them isn't much fun.

"You don't really think Mama let Mr. Tricks out, right?" I asked.

She folded up the facecloth. "I don't know why I said that," she say softly.

If that was an apology for what she say about Mama, it was good enough for me. I didn't want to stay mad at Meadow Lark.

Then, as if the subject were closed, she say, "I got something from my dad today."

Meadow Lark opened her bureau drawer and pulled out a sheet of paper and waved it at me. "He sent me a letter." It was on the same crinkly paper as his first letter, so I guessed it was also typewritten.

"Oh, that's nice," I say, and reached for it.

But she slid it back into the drawer. "I'll let you read it later," she say, and sniffed toward the hall. "*Mmm.* Your mom's such a good cook."

"It's because Daddy's home. And we better go down now."

"Wait," Meadow Lark say. "She might want these." She reached under her bed and pulled out the Tupperware she brought with her and carried it down to the kitchen.

Inside were two dozen yeast rolls, the kind made with soft white flour and butter. And even after being in there for nearly a week under her bed, they looked as fresh as if they'd just come out of the oven.

Mama brought out her special bread basket,

which she lined with a white cloth napkin. Then Meadow Lark placed the rolls in it. "My dad told me to bring them," she explained.

Mama smiled. "How nice of him."

"And he sent her a letter," I say.

"To our post office box," Meadow Lark added quickly, and put the last roll in the basket. "We're still getting settled."

"Well, then," Mama say, "since you're getting to know your way around, remember to stay away from that river."

We both nodded and she picked up the basket, then sniffed the air. "You two smell like Ivory now," she say, and went to the dining room.

Meadow Lark and I glanced at each other, and I could tell by her expression that she was thinking about the river and that log stuck in the mud and the next time we'd be able to go see it—just like I was.

The dining table looked like a holiday, gleaming with the real silverware and Mama's good crystal and her plates with the gold trim, all set on her white tablecloth. Mama's good platter piled with pot roast cut into chunks sat in the center, surrounded by the dishes of green beans and whipped potatoes, her silver gravy boat, and the basket of Meadow Lark's rolls. And Mama was wearing red lipstick. She had lit two tall candles, and their flames stretched and flickered, and the room held its breath as if waiting for some wonderful, shiny thing to happen.

Everything looked so good and cheerful, the way every day should be. But it wasn't perfect, because the chair next to Meadow Lark was still empty. No matter how pretty Mama set the table, or how good the food smelled, that beautiful scene wasn't complete without Theron sitting in that chair.

I looked down at my lap, because I didn't want anyone to see me looking sad. My heart hurt for Mama, that she had put so much trouble into making that table so beautiful, but no matter how hard she tried, she couldn't make it perfect. If the meal had been shabby, maybe seeing that empty seat wouldn't have felt so sharp.

Daddy didn't seem to notice, and he lifted his glass of wine to Mama. She passed Meadow Lark the potatoes piled high in a gold-rim bowl. They were so smooth that when Meadow Lark plunked out a spoonful, they flattened on her plate.

"Whereabouts in Arizona are you from?" Daddy asked as he forked a chunk of roast onto his plate.

"Near Phoenix, out in the desert," Meadow Lark say. I'd already told them where she was from, so I knew Daddy was being polite by asking her directly.

Meadow Lark poured gravy on her potatoes. She didn't know enough to make a well in them first, and the gravy pooled around them, touching the green beans.

Then she put the gravy boat back on the table so gently that it didn't make a noise on the tablecloth, the same way she opened Theron's door so quietly that you knew she'd opened many doors that way before.

"There aren't any rivers in Arizona," I say.

"Oh, yes, there are," Daddy say.

Mama passed me the platter of pot roast. "Help yourself, River."

Meadow Lark sat chewing and looking at her plate, and I tried again. "Daddy, you've been to Phoenix. You go there all the time for work."

Daddy smiled at me and swallowed. "I don't go that far west very often," he say, and at that I decided to stop talking, so he wouldn't contradict me anymore. Meadow Lark, not me and not the pot roast, appeared to be the center of attention.

Mama held the bread basket out to Meadow Lark and unfolded the white napkin like a rose. "Have one of your rolls, dear," she say. "How nice of your father to make them."

"Oh, he didn't make them," Meadow Lark say.

She chose one and put it on her plate. "We got them at the Bread Box."

Mama took one out of the basket. "Hmm," she say, examining it. "Well, it was thoughtful of him anyway."

Then Mama put the roll on her plate in a way I knew meant she wouldn't be picking it up again, not trusting where it come from.

I took one too. It was all part of forgiving Meadow Lark.

"Did you ever go to the trolley museum in Phoenix?" Daddy asked, lifting a fork of green beans. By then I'd stopped listening to Daddy talk about Arizona and the mountains and the museums in Phoenix. Something more interesting was going on right in front of me. Mama was staring at Meadow Lark, studying her, as if she were waiting for Meadow Lark to do something astounding, like catch fire.

"Butter?" Mama asked, holding out the butter plate to Meadow Lark.

Meadow Lark put a pale little square on her plate. She picked up the roll from the gold-rim plate glimmering with candlelight.

When Meadow Lark picked up the roll, Mama say, "I—you—" but her breathing sounded short and quick, like she was inhaling snow crystals, and she didn't finish what she started to say.

Meadow Lark touched the roll with the fingers of her other hand. Outside, the blanket of cloud pulled away from a soft, coral sky. Soon it would be time to sit out with Daddy and listen and wait.

"They used to have mules pull the trolleys," he was saying. "It took three hours to make all the stops down through the city."

Meadow Lark tore off a piece of roll, and Mama put her hand to her mouth.

"What, Mama?" I asked.

Daddy stopped talking about Arizona and mules and looked at Mama. "Dear?" he say.

"I'm . . . ," Mama's eyes grew wide and glittery in the candlelight, and her lips made a red O.

"What is it, Caroline?" Daddy asked, but Mama just kept looking at Meadow Lark like she was seeing her again after a very long time.

Then she stood up. "Excuse me," she say, and left the dining room, touching Meadow Lark's shoulder on the way out.

The three of us sat there looking at one another for the longest time, as if we expected Mama to come back in with dessert. Finally, I asked, "What was she talking about, Daddy?"

"I think she's just tired," he say, and then he excused himself and went upstairs.

Meadow Lark and I looked at each other. She ate until her plate was clean, and when she helped herself to more beans, I went up to Mama's room.

She lay flat on their bed like a plunk of whipped potatoes, her dark hair spilling off the pillow, and her lipstick a red smudge on her mouth.

"Mama?" I asked. She touched my arm and say very gently, "I'm fine, honey. Just let me alone a while."

"I told her she needed to see the doctor," Daddy say, but Mama shook her head.

"I'm just fine, Ingram," she say, and looked at the doorway. "Where's your friend? Where's Meadow Lark?"

"She's still eating," I say.

Mama smiled. "She's a nice girl. You two do the dishes. I'll be down in a while."

Then she and Daddy shared another one of those looks that didn't need words, and Daddy kissed her forehead. "Let's go, River," he say to me, and ushered me out to the hall and closed the door softly.

"What's wrong with her?" I asked.

"I don't know. Did Meadow Lark say something that upset her?"

I went over in my mind what happened just before Mama left the table. Mama served the food, and Meadow Lark started eating one of her rolls, and then suddenly Mama acted funny.

"I don't think so," I say, but something about those moments just before Mama left the table—like the hushed moments in church—felt like held breath. Maybe Mama saw something she'd been looking for. I just didn't know what.

"Maybe Mama will explain it to us," I say to Daddy.

Mama was on my mind all during the time Meadow Lark and I washed the dishes and when we sat out with Daddy in silence. Silence is different from quiet, because quiet is peaceful, and all during the dusk time my mind churned with questions.

What happened to Mama?

Did she see something?

What?

Question after question come to me, each one leading to the next, until finally I asked, *What does Meadow Lark have to do with it?*

Chapter 14

I lay awake almost the whole night, first looking at the ceiling, then looking at the wall, then out the window, and then at Meadow Lark, who sighed every so often in her sleep.

Ever since she come to school two weeks ago, strange things started happening. First we met at the river, then we found that pretty white feather, we wished for Daniel Bunch to go away, then Daniel Bunch got sick, we found Mr. Tricks and brought him here, and then he disappeared. I knew there was something different, extraordinary, about Meadow Lark, but no one else noticed that until tonight when she tore that roll. Mama recognized it too. Or maybe Mama only wished she had.

Thoughts like that kept me awake most of that night. In the dark, your mind can talk you into believing lots of things that you would laugh about during the day. I was a breath away from convincing myself that Meadow Lark was more than an ordinary girl, when she turned over and did a little snore and then her stomach gurgled, and I was assured that she was a very ordinary girl, just like me.

I knew Mama was fine, because Daddy was with her. I heard him talking to her after he say good night to me and Meadow Lark. I couldn't hear the words, but his voice stretched like a kitten reaching for a warm patch. Though my ears strained to hear Mama's voice, she never spoke.

This never would have happened if Theron were still here. If he were still here, Daniel wouldn't talk to me the way he did, I probably wouldn't have become friends with Meadow Lark, and then she wouldn't have come to stay with us. That's how time works— one thing happens and leads to another and then another, all in order like pearls on a string. But if the string breaks, the pearls fall off and roll around and what happened next and why get all mixed up. And it's really hard to string them again in the same order, especially if some have rolled away.

There was a string that stretched between the day Theron left and this night when I lay awake, and all the pearls had fallen to the floor. If I were to put them back, what order would I string them?

Theron leaves us. Theron and Daddy argue.

Theron say he's going away and never coming back, and don't bother looking for him. Theron leaves us. Theron crashes the car into the river. Theron gets drunk—so they say. Theron gives Daniel a ride home. Theron leaves us. Theron meets up with his friends. I start talking funny. Mama sees something when she looks at Meadow Lark. Theron leaves us.

The pearl I kept picking up was the Theron-leaves-us one, but I never want that pearl. If that one rolled away, time from that night when Theron crashed the car to this night would look very different. How I wished Theron hadn't left.

Sometime that night, Meadow Lark got out of bed and went into the bathroom. She come back after a while. But then I must have fallen asleep, and here's what made that a strange night—the next time I looked over at her bed, it was empty, and I heard a noise.

"Meadow Lark?" I say softly, but she didn't answer.

I heard the noise again—a soft thud, like a drawer closing somewhere outside our bedroom.

I got up and walked out to the hall, and listened. I heard the noise again. It come from Theron's room.

His door was ajar, so I pushed it open. "Meadow Lark?" I say again.

There she was, standing in front of his bureau and staring at herself as if she didn't hear me. The moonlight through the window wove through her nightgown and hair, which was all puffed out from sleeping. The sight of her made me shiver.

Is this what Mama saw? I wondered. *Some kind of ghost?*

"Meadow Lark, are you awake?" I asked, and when she still didn't answer me, I decided she was sleepwalking again. "Let's go back to our room. It's the middle of the night."

"Mr. Tricks," she say. "Where is he?" she asked.

She turned to me, and in the moonlight her eye looked wide and confused. Scared, I stepped back.

"Do you know where he is?" she asked.

"No, I don't," I say, as if she could be awake. "But this is Theron's room, and he's not in here."

"But I looked everywhere else for him. Someone let him go."

Oh no—not Mama again, I thought, my heart thumping.

"Did you let him go?"

"No, I didn't. Did you?" I asked, waving my hand in front of her face. "Are you just pretending?" I asked. "Are you really awake? Because this isn't funny, Meadow Lark."

"Did you take him down to the river?" she asked me. "Everything ends up in the river."

"Let's talk about this tomorrow, okay?" I say. Seeing her in the moonlight like that gave me goose bumps. I had to get her back to our room without waking her up, so I circled my arms to herd her toward the door.

To my surprise, Meadow Lark walked out of the room. I looked around once more to make sure everything was the way it was supposed to be. Theron's sweatshirt hung over the doorknob to his closet, and his sneakers lay crossways on his rug, and the picture of Shawna sat on the bureau, right next to his trophy . . . but his trophy was gone!

"Meadow Lark, did you . . . ," I started to ask, but decided to wait until the morning, when she was awake.

She was in bed when I got back to our room, with her eyes closed, looking fast asleep as if she had never gotten up. I sat on my bed for a few minutes and watched her.

After a few minutes I lay down, shivering over what had happened. She was so attached to Mr. Tricks that she thought about him even while she slept. He followed her around and ate carrots from her finger, and she puckered her lips to him. Of course she missed him.

Meadow Lark's bed creaked. I tensed, ready to peel back my covers and settle her back down. But she just rolled over onto her side. Soon her breathing sounded soft and smooth, and I knew she would stay there for the rest of the night.

I counted to a hundred, until I was sure she wouldn't get out of bed again, and then I got the flashlight from my bureau drawer and tiptoed back to Theron's room to look for his trophy.

I looked on his bureau and on his desk. In his closet, on every shelf and behind the hanging clothes. On the bed, on the bookshelf, behind the door, in every drawer in his room, and under his bed and his night table. I looked until I was sadly assured that his trophy was not in his room.

With his trophy missing, a piece of Theron had gone too. And now, the world felt off, twisted, and spun away from its orbit. I feared that one after another, pieces of him would disappear, taking Theron with them, until one day he would be gone from us completely and forever. And then one morning the sun wouldn't rise.

I went back to bed, and next thing I knew it was morning, and as I woke up, I smelled rain outside. This was going to be a wet summer.

When I opened my eyes, I looked over to Meadow Lark's bed. She was quietly writing on a napkin with a red pen. She made two marks and folded the napkin into quarters, and then she slipped the napkin into her back pocket. That's when I discovered that Meadow Lark drew her own red hearts.

I closed my eyes and heard her get up and leave the room, shutting the door softly. I listened for her footsteps down the stairs, and then got out of bed and slid open her bottom drawer. There I saw a handful of white paper napkins, the kind Mama keeps in the napkin holder on the table, next to a few sheets of thin paper with typewriting on them — the letters from her daddy. Maybe Theron's trophy was in there too, I thought, and rummaged around. But it wasn't there.

As I closed the drawer, I become aware of two things: the smell of maple-cured bacon and a sound I hadn't heard for months — Mama humming in the kitchen.

I raced down to the kitchen to give Mama a big hug, and then stopped — she and Meadow Lark were there together, and Mama was humming as she twisted Meadow Lark's hair into a tight bun at the back of her head.

"There," she say, smoothing down some loose strands. "That will keep the smell out of your hair."

"Thanks," Meadow Lark say. Then she picked up

a fork and turned a strip of bacon in the fry pan.

"Use the tongs, or you'll burn yourself," I say, repeating what Mama had always told me.

"She can use a fork if she wants to," Mama say, and went back to humming.

"Why are you doing that, Mama?" I asked.

Mama opened a cupboard door. "Doing what?"

"Humming. You haven't done that since—"

"Can't I hum?"

I looked at Mama and then at Meadow Lark, and I didn't like what I saw. "No, it make my bones itch."

"It *makes* your bones itch, River," Mama say, with that purple-plum look on her face.

"And Meadow Lark, you have to stop walking in your sleep. *And*—" I was just about to tell her she had to stay out of Theron's room, but I stopped myself because Mama would be upset to hear that.

Meadow Lark turned another piece of bacon in the fry pan. "I was sleepwalking?" she asked. "When?"

"Last night. You don't remember?"

"You have to be careful on the stairs," Mama say. "We can put up a railing so you don't fall."

"I don't remember that," Meadow Lark say to me. "What did I do?"

Just then the bacon spit out of the pan. "Ouch!" she cried, and touched her arm.

"Oh, dear. I'll get you something for that," Mama say, and left the kitchen.

While Mama was in the bathroom, I whispered to Meadow Lark, "You were in Theron's room last night."

"I was? I don't remember that at all." She turned back to the fry pan.

"Theron's trophy isn't in his room. Do you know where it is? Did you take it?"

Mama come back with some cooling ointment and a bandage. "Show me where it hurts," she say, and fixed up Meadow Lark's arm. I waited the whole time for Meadow Lark to answer my question.

When Mama was done, Meadow Lark say, "Well, I can't be responsible for what I do in my sleep."

"No one can," Mama say, and pat the bandage over her arm. "There, you'll feel better in no time."

"And if I can't be responsible for what I do in my sleep," Meadow Lark say, hitching a strand of her hair behind her ear and looking me straight in the eye, "then anything is possible."

Chapter 15

I was in the art room when my mind went back to that house.

Next time, try to stay longer and see what happens, Meadow Lark had told me. Well, here I was, at the bottom of the staircase, so I started climbing it. Mint-green wallpaper with dark ferns covered the walls from the first floor to the ceiling of the second floor. Halfway up to the second floor, the staircase took a sharp turn and curled around all the way to the top.

As usual, the house was quiet. All those times I had gone there and sat in that kitchen and smelled that pantry, and walked around the dining room and run my fingers across that carved table, and pushed the keys on the adding machine, I had never seen one person.

There was no sound—no bacon sizzling or mama humming—and I wondered if anyone lived in that big, quiet house.

When I reached the top of the stairs, I saw a long

hallway with a window at the end. A carpet like the
one in the dining room, with swirls and flowers and
fringe, ran the length of the hallway. In front of me
was a bedroom that had a dark wood floor with marks
on it, as if people had walked on it wearing sharp
heels or had dragged heavy old furniture across it.
The room had the same tall windows as downstairs,
with long, dark curtains that blocked out the sunlight. A big poster bed, with a carved pineapple on
each post, was pushed against the wall. It had a bedspread like Mama's, only pink, and when I ran my
hand over it, my fingers buzzed.

The smell of lilacs filled the room, and on the tall,
dark bureau was a brush with a nest of brown hairs
the color of maple syrup, and a matching comb stuck
in its bristles. A bottle of perfume rested on a round
mirrored tray with two earrings like gold knots, and
beside the tray sat a music box that looked just like
mine. When I opened it, the ballerina twirled around
and the box played a tune that Mama used to call
"Some Enchanted Evening."

Just like my box, this one was full of jewelry and
other things. This box held three tarnished pennies,
some colored pebbles, and a plastic barrette with strands
of brown hair stuck in it. I also saw a copper-colored
chain, a handful of earrings that didn't match, a pin

that looked like an artist's easel, and another pin that sparkled.

My fingers smelled like metal, and I kept digging. In the bottom, under all those things, I found an oval locket, as small as my pinkie nail, with a picture of a baby inside. I took the locket out of the box and set it on the bureau. Then I lifted the tray.

"River?" Ms. Zucchero say, back in the art room. In an instant that house, the music, and that tiny picture of the baby vanished. For the first time since I started going to that house, I didn't want to leave it. Everything disappeared but the smell of lilacs, which lingered in the art room and tickled my nose.

"Are you all done?" she asked.

It was lunch period, and because Daniel had ruined my first collage, I had come into the art room to work on a second one.

"Almost," I say, and noticed a bouquet of lilacs spilling over the lip of a clear vase on her desk. They replaced the pink carnations from her brother, which had wilted. I hoped the lilacs come from Mr. Sievers.

Ms. Zucchero walked over to the art table. "You did a great job of re-creating it. I'm so sorry about what Daniel did to the first one. I should have made quiet time before that happened."

I knew she felt bad, so I shook my head. "It wasn't your fault," I say. The only person who should have felt bad didn't.

"I'm really glad to see that you and Meadow Lark are friends. I don't know her well, but I think she needs a friend like you."

Lately, Meadow Lark hadn't needed me at all. She and Mama seemed fine without me ever since that morning at breakfast. Now, Mama was always asking Meadow Lark if she slept well or had enough to eat or needed any help with her homework, and yesterday Mama bought a family-size bag of Cheetos.

"No one knows her very well," I say, "her being new."

"Like me," Ms. Zucchero say. "So I know what it's like to be the new person."

"Well, you have a friend who give you flowers, right?" I was afraid that might be too personal, but when she laughed, I knew it wasn't.

"The lilacs are from my landlady's garden. She let me pick as many as I wanted."

Then Ms. Zucchero leaned closer to my collage, and I knew the personal subject was closed. "You know, this one is even better than the first," she say.

I stared at the new collage. "Well, it took me less time to make than the first one. Maybe because I didn't have to figure it all out again the second time."

She smiled. "Sometimes it happens that way." Then she pointed to one of the pieces of colored glass. "That's so pretty."

"I liked how the water made it look like a jewel."

Then she pointed to the bald plastic baby, being careful not to touch it. The black paint that Daniel threw on the collage had soaked into the bottom part of the baby, making it look like it was wearing pants.

"Tell me the story behind this," she say.

"Well, I don't know what kind of story there is to tell. I found it stuck between some rocks at the river. They wouldn't let it go until I picked it up."

Ms. Zucchero slid out a stool and sat on it. "And what made you pick it up?"

In my mind I saw the little plastic baby stuck in the rocks, with the water pouring over it.

"Because it was there. Because . . . I don't know why."

I stopped talking and shook my head, still seeing that baby in the river, and I couldn't tell her why I picked it up.

But Ms. Zucchero wouldn't accept that. "Lots of things must have been there. But why did you choose this?"

"I just liked it." I knew that was the easy answer, and we had a reason why we put every one of those things on our collages.

But Ms. Zucchero kept asking me about that baby. "There isn't another reason?"

I remembered that baby in the water, with its little plastic arms up. "I picked it up because the water was covering it. That baby looked like it was drowning . . . and I'm afraid of the water. I didn't want to see it drown."

Ms. Zucchero nodded and say, "I see."

I wasn't sure Ms. Zucchero did see. She didn't come to the school until after Theron left, and she come from Virginia, where she wouldn't have known anything about him or what happened to our family since then. So I kept talking about the plastic baby. "And I picked it up because someone had lost it."

"I think you're right, River."

I touched the plastic baby glued to the collage. "I picked it up because it needed me to find it."

The stool screeched on the floor as Ms. Zucchero stood up. "That's a great story, River," she say. "I loved hearing it. One day I want to hear your story."

"My story? I don't have one."

"Everyone has a story," she say, and went back to her desk.

I looked at my collage again. *Maybe when Mama sees it,* I thought, *she will twist my hair into a bun and hum beside me in the kitchen.*

"Please put it on the wall with the others, so everyone can see it. Don't worry, it'll be safe." I knew she meant because Daniel wasn't around.

I started putting away the glue and scissors and pens, thinking about how that baby needed me to find it. It wanted me to find it.

I picked up the scraps of paper and brushed the crumbs of glue and eraser into my hand, and froze, as a thought swooped down on me:

Theron needs me to find him.

"River, are you all right?"

"Yes, I'm fine."

I thought about that as I carried the scraps to the bin, my mind racing. Even if Theron didn't want me to find him, maybe he needed me to.

Or maybe the truth was that I needed to find him. And, somehow, I would.

Chapter 16

"Here's some news that will make Sonya happy," Kevin Kale say in art class later that afternoon. "Bunch is out of the hospital."

"That's not news," Sonya say. I noticed the flutter that was in her voice the day Daniel Bunch went into the hospital was all gone. I liked her better when she worried about Daniel.

Meadow Lark would say that wish had brought Daniel Bunch back from the brink of death. I say it was just a coincidence. In either case, I needed to see for myself that he was home, and I needed to see that today.

"Are you sure?" I asked.

"Can someone keep her quiet? That girl talks too much," Sonya say, turning to me. "And why are you so interested in Daniel? I have it on the best authority, namely Daniel himself, that he hates you. So stop talking about him. In fact, why don't you not talk at all."

Poor Sonya, I thought. How could anyone have a crush on Daniel Bunch?

"Everyone," Ms. Zucchero say from her desk, "we're going to start our final project tomorrow, so please take your collages home today."

After the last bell rang, instead of waiting for Meadow Lark, I started walking in the direction of Daniel's house. It had started to sprinkle again, so I tucked my collage under my shirt to keep it dry.

"River, wait!" Meadow Lark called from the steps. "Where are you going?"

"I'll be home later," I say, but waited for her to catch up.

"Can I come?" she asked.

I shook my head. "I have to go by myself."

"But where are you going?"

I stared at Meadow Lark, then say, "Promise you won't tell anyone."

She crossed her heart. "Promise." Then her good eye got wide behind her blue-framed glasses and she say, "Hey, I heard Daniel Bunch is out of the hospital."

"That's where I'm going . . . to see him for myself."

Meadow Lark put her hand to her mouth. "So you know what that means. . . . Our wish—it worked."

"I have to go now," I say. I didn't want to talk

about wishes or miracles or coincidences. "Don't tell anyone, remember?"

"But what if your mama asks?"

"*Especially* don't tell Mama."

Daniel Bunch's little sister answered the door, holding a bowl of cherries. Cherry juice ran all down her chin and stained her T-shirt in the shape of New Jersey. Her smile revealed a missing front tooth, and her gray neck had pale patches, as if she'd tried to scrub her skin.

She held out the bowl to me. "I'm Honor. Want some?"

I slid my collage out from my shirt and leaned it behind a chair on the porch. It would be safer there than inside, close to Daniel Bunch.

"Take one," she say again.

I shook my head. "No, thanks." There was no telling where those cherries had been.

Then she stuck the bowl right under my nose. "You have to. It's the law."

I took two and closed my hand around them. She kept looking at me, so I say, "I just ate, so I'll save them. Is your brother home?"

"Well . . . ," she say, looking behind her. "Are you a tutor?"

"Tutor? . . . N-no."

"My brother wants a tutor," she whispered.

Then she pointed to the living room. "He's in there trying to do homework."

I took a deep breath and went into the living room. It smelled like overripe fruit.

Daniel Bunch sat slumped into the sofa in a rumpled-up T-shirt and shorts, his feet flat on the coffee table, with a book open in his lap. His left arm rested on a rolled-up blanket beside him. Daniel Bunch looked like a skeleton in clothes, his shoulder bones poking through his shirt.

He glared at me as I come in, then looked back down at his book. "What are you here for?" he asked. "To finish the job?"

I took another breath, then exhaled the quivers. Tucked into the sofa with the back of his T-shirt pushed up his neck, Daniel Bunch looked like a curled-over old man. And if Meadow Lark was right and the only reason he come home from the hospital from the edge of the death was because of us, he should have been grateful.

"I just come to see you," I say in a voice I hoped sounded confident.

"Well, you saw me," he say. "Now get out."

My heartbeat sped up and my leg muscles

twitched. I wanted to run, but instead I stumbled back into a big, soft chair across from Daniel.

He tossed his book on the table with a clap and asked, "Why *did* you come? Did my sister check you for weapons first?"

"I wasn't trying to kill you in the hospital. I was —"

"I wake up and you're holding a knife in my face, and that's not trying to kill me?"

" — trying to see if you were breathing. You looked dead. Even Benjamin say so."

"Benjamin? What *are* you talking about?"

"That boy across the hall from you."

"Never met him," he say.

"Really? Because he seemed to know you."

"Whatever," he say, and waved Benjamin away. "As you can see, I'm not dead."

Daniel shut his eyes and threw his head back against the sofa. My heartbeat returned to normal. Daniel looked too skinny and weak to scare me the way he did at school, and today he didn't even want to try.

"School's almost over. Are you coming back?" I asked.

He let out a big sigh that sounded like, *Why must I put up with you?*

"Are you going to graduate sixth grade?"

Then Daniel Bunch shocked me because instead of glaring or telling me to mind my own business, he looked down at his book and shrugged, and wriggled his bony-white toes on his bony-white feet and say, "I don't know."

"Really? They might not graduate you from sixth?" I almost added "either," but at the moment, he looked too pitiful.

"Maybe," he mumbled.

I watched his toes wriggle for a few seconds, and then my gaze drifted to the notebook beside his feet and some words written there in his rat-scratch scrawl:

I wish I had a tutor.

So, Honor had told the truth when she say that Daniel wanted a tutor.

I knew his secret, and, feeling bold, I asked, "What are you flunking?"

He flattened the book on his legs and pushed his head back against the sofa and sighed. But his toes kept wriggling, and finally he say, "Just name it."

One of Mama's sayings come to me at that moment, the one about being kind to your enemies. I crossed my legs and draped my elbows on the arms of the big chair. "You could go to summer school . . . or you could get a tutor, right?"

For a moment he looked surprised, but the old Daniel Bunch come right back when he looked at me like I was stupid. "Too late," he say, as he slid the notebook off the table with his foot.

"Well, it's too bad my brother's not here to help," I say, to uncover his secret wish.

Then he picked up his book again and pretended to read. I could tell because his eyes moved across the same place over and over. "What are you talking about?"

"My brother is a good tutor," I say, remembering the jobs he did to buy his Giant.

Daniel touched his wrist cast. "Was," he say.

"How do you . . . ?"

"He used to tutor me."

Theron—tutored Daniel? "Theron never told—" I started to say, but Daniel interrupted me.

"But he can't anymore because now he's a fugitive."

It could have been a real conversation with Daniel. We might have been able to figure out the problem between us, but he destroyed that moment, just like he destroyed my collage. "You need to get your facts straight, Daniel Bunch," I say, sitting straight in the chair. "He wasn't even arrested."

"Then why did he run away?"

"People run away for lots of reasons. . . . They're

mad or scared or . . . they feel bad," I say, remembering what Theron say just before he left us.

*I'm leaving. But I'm never coming back, so don't look
for me.*

I continued. "No wonder you're flunking everything. You don't even know the difference between
getting convicted and being accused—*falsely* accused!"
I say, and realized my foot was jiggling.

"Get out of here!" Daniel yelled. "No one asked
you here."

He looked so weak in his rumpled-up, torn clothes
and his bony-white feet on the coffee table. *Don't be
scared of him,* I kept telling myself as I stood up to leave.

Just then Honor come into the living room holding my collage. She still had that bowl of cherries in
the other hand. "Is this yours?" she asked. "It might
get wet outside."

Great, I thought. *Now Daniel will see it.*

"Thanks," I say, and took it from her.

"Let's see that," Daniel say. "Come on—what is it?"

"You know, Daniel."

"I thought I destroyed that . . . in an *accident.*"

"Well, you didn't," I say, and thrust it in front of
him so he could get a good look.

Daniel Bunch sat back against the cushions
and folded his arms in front of him and studied the

collage. Then he put his hand to his chin and a little smile come to his mouth. "Yup, it stinks."

Daniel still had the power to make me feel like a crushed-up soda can, but I looked down so he wouldn't see.

"No it doesn't," Honor say.

I smiled at her, at her dirty neck and her stained shirt, for keeping me from crying in front of Daniel.

"You just don't have any taste," she say.

"And you're stupid, stupid," he say back.

"He calls me that all the time because he doesn't know many other words," Honor whispered to me. Then she held out the cherry bowl, and this time I took a handful.

"Daniel," I asked, "why do you hate me so much?"

"Now what are you talking about?" he say, and turned back to his book.

I waited for his answer. And waited some more, and then I asked, "Well, why?"

"Well, nothing. *Now* get out — or I'll kick you out."

I whirled around toward the front door and started to leave. Then Daniel did something surprising. He actually say my name, "River," and when I turned around, Daniel looked at me, his face so red and wide-eyed that it was hard to believe it belonged to Daniel. "Ask your brother. That's why."

Theron. What did Theron have to do with why Daniel hated me? For a second, Daniel made me think that it could be that easy—that I could go home and ask Theron why. But just as fast, a sadness thick as mud pressed on my heart, and I say, "I only wish I could."

Chapter 17

It was still sprinkling when I left Daniel's house, and I tucked my collage under my shirt to keep it dry. Even though the rain was soft and warm, I shivered. Daniel say that Theron tutored him. What else didn't I know about my brother? What else didn't I know about Daniel?

I wish I had a tutor, Daniel had scrawled in his notebook. Everyone has a wish, even Daniel, and knowing that made my heart a little softer for him. Caring about other people hurts, I discovered, because your heart breaks with theirs.

I could try being nicer to Daniel and he'd never need to know. He wanted a tutor. I could make that wish for him. Meadow Lark would say she had convinced me that those wishes we floated down the river come true, but she hadn't. I just wanted to do for Daniel what he couldn't do for himself right now. That is, if he even knew about floating wishes down the river.

Wishes—I had so many of my own, and as I

walked to the river, they all pushed one another aside in my mind, jostling for my attention:

I wish Mr. Tricks is alive and his wing is healed.

I wish he would come back to Meadow Lark, because she really loves that pidge.

I wish Theron is safe and happy.

I wish Mama would smooth my hair into a ponytail.

I wish Daddy would go to Boston more often, instead of Chicago or Orlando or St. Louis.

I wish Theron misses us.

I wish for a little red heart on my napkin.

I wish Daniel would be nicer.

I wish Mama would like the collage.

I wish Theron wants us to find him.

I wish Meadow Lark would go home so Mama wouldn't pay so much attention to her.

I wish Meadow Lark and I could be best friends again.

I wish Daniel would tell me more about Theron.

I wish Theron would come home.

I couldn't count the number of times each day my heart made that last wish.

By then I had reached the sandy beach. I looked at the river flowing by, imagining myself stepping out there. I remembered how it felt to wake up and feel the river curling around my legs, and I knew I couldn't go out into the water.

But I could go directly to the log and put his wish on it. So I picked my way through the woods to the little cove, and when I reached the log, I noticed something looked different about it. When Meadow Lark and I first found the log, it was stuck firmly into the riverbank and angled upstream. Now it stretched three or four feet farther out over the water and pointed downstream.

Carefully I stepped to where the log met the riverbank, and crouched to get a better look. And blinked. Our three wishes had grown into thirty, all fluttering on the log. It was a collage of wishes. No one else knew about wishing on the river or about the log, so Meadow Lark must have put these wishes here.

Shadows from the opposite bank had reached all the way across the river, calling dusk to settle. Quickly I wrote Daniel's wish for a tutor on a scrap of paper and tossed it into the water in front of the log, and hoped that the log would catch it.

Just as I turned to leave, I saw something floating in the air from across the river. Closer and closer it come, as if it knew my scent. It was a white feather.

I reached out and closed my hand around it, and tucked it into my pocket.

Wishes floated everywhere.

Chapter 18

Our house smelled like butter and vanilla and warm sugar when I got home from the river. I followed the scent to the kitchen, where I found two layers of yellow cake cooling on the table and Meadow Lark wearing Daddy's Minnesota apron.

"What are you doing?" I asked, hearing my voice flutter.

Meadow Lark picked up a big bowl of lemon frosting. "Your mama and I made a cake," she say, and stirred the frosting with Mama's big spoon.

"But Mama and I always make that cake," I say, and turned to Mama. "Don't we?" But she was busy pulling out the frosting spreader from the knife drawer.

"I'm sorry, honey," she say. "Meadow Lark wanted to make a cake. . . ."

"And we didn't know when you'd be home," Meadow Lark say, staring at me and stirring.

"You couldn't wait for me?" I whined.

"Meadow Lark didn't know where you were. And I didn't know where you were," Mama say.

"It's just a cake," Meadow Lark say.

I felt my eyes narrow and my pulse drumbeat my neck. Mama and Meadow Lark were becoming best friends, and that hurt. "It's not just a cake. It's the cake Mama and I make every summer."

"Grab a knife, River," Mama say cheerily. "You can help us frost it. . . . Where were you, anyway?"

The collage under my shirt felt tight around my chest as I looked at the two of them. I didn't want to help them frost the cake. And I didn't want to give Mama the collage. She didn't need it, she probably wouldn't even want it . . . and why was Meadow Lark staring at me?

"Never mind," I say, and ran up the stairs, shutting the door loud enough for anyone to hear. Then I pulled the collage out and slid it in the back of my closet.

First, I thought as I fell on the bed, Meadow Lark took over my place at the river. Next, she took over my bedroom. All her stuff—her duffel bag, her backpack, her Arizona bag, that Tupperware that started Mama humming again, her shoes on the floor and clothes hanging from the bedposts—had started creeping over to my side. But now, worse than either of those, now she was taking over Mama.

I gazed at the ceiling. Meadow Lark had slipped perfectly into my life, and no one seemed to notice the difference. What would she take over next?

Footsteps thudded in the hall of that house in my mind. I stood in front of the tall bureau, my hand on the ballerina box. I had to see what was under the tray, because I knew it was important, but the footsteps got closer, louder. I would have to move fast.

Quickly I lifted the tray and peeked inside the box. There, all by itself, was a folded-up yellow tissue. The footsteps were almost at the door.

I grabbed the box and slipped under the bed. The bedspread hung low enough to hide me, and I slid all the way over to the wall.

The footsteps stopped. I held my breath and peeked through the fringe of the bedspread. At the doorway stood two feet wearing fluffy blue bedroom shoes.

My heart pounded, and a gasp worked its way up my throat. I pressed the tissue to my mouth to muffle anything that come out of my mouth.

She walked over to the bureau, and then I heard that crunchy sound of hair brushing. *Please don't notice that the ballerina box is gone*, I thought. Then she put the hairbrush down, and opened and shut a drawer. "Naptime's over," she say, as if to herself, and walked out of the room and down the hall.

My heart was racing, but I sat very still until the house quieted down again. The folded-up tissue had gotten soggy from my breath, and flakes of it stuck to my hand. Something hard and round was inside. Carefully I unfolded the tissue.

There, all by itself, lay a little gold ring with an emerald on it. It was just like the one in my ballerina box, just like the one I found at the river.

Something so very strange happened then. That pretty little ring meant for a baby, which shouldn't have fit on my pinkie, now slid easily onto my ring finger.

I blinked and realized I'd been staring at the ceiling all that time. The house and the blue bedroom shoes and the little emerald ring stayed fresh in my mind.

That ring had slipped on my ring finger so easily. I got up to try it again, and opened my ballerina box. My ring wasn't on top. I rummaged through the box, but my little emerald ring wasn't in it.

It had to be there, so I dumped the box onto my bed, and spread out all the coins and broken brace-lets and bobby pins and rocks. I reached over and turned on the lamp to get a better look. There was no ring on my bed and no ring in my box.

I went to the bathroom and pulled out drawers and shelves. No ring.

The last time I saw the ring was when I showed it to Meadow Lark, the same day she showed me her letter from her daddy.

Just then, she come in and flopped down on her bed. "We're done. Your mama said the cake is for dessert. Hey, what are you doing? Are you okay?" she say all at once.

I was sitting on my bed, surrounded by everything I'd dumped out of my drawers and my ballerina box.

"Did you see my ring?" I asked. "My little emerald ring that I showed you. I can't find it."

"No," she say and shook her head. "I haven't seen it. You lost that pretty ring? Did you look in your drawers? In the bathroom? Under your bed?"

"I looked everywhere," I say, trying so hard to keep the tears where they belonged, but two of them popped out before I could look away from Meadow Lark.

"River?"

I brushed at the tears. "It has to be here somewhere."

"I'll help you look," she say, getting off the bed.

"No, I can do it. You don't need to help." When I

say that, I realized there was more to my tears than losing the ring.

"River, you're not mad at me, are you—for making the cake with your mama?"

"Why did you do that?" I asked, wiping my cheeks.

"Well," she say, sitting back on the bed, "I was trying to think of a way to distract her, so she wouldn't wonder where you were."

I picked up my pillow and hugged it. That sounded like she just made it up, but I say, "Thanks. I didn't think of that."

"Well, if anything bothers you, you have to tell me, okay? We're best friends."

I nodded.

"Good," she say, and pulled a half bag of pretzel sticks from under her bed. "So, how is Daniel?"

"He looked like a skeleton. And being sick didn't make him any nicer."

"Why—did he hurt you?" she asked, holding a pretzel stick in the air like it was a sword.

I couldn't help but smile. "No," I say. "Daniel couldn't even get himself off the sofa. I felt sorry for him a little. I even show him my collage . . ."

But I couldn't finish, couldn't tell her that Daniel say it still stunk. That was not funny, and I hugged my pillow tighter.

"Then I went down to the river . . . and the log. And Meadow Lark, there were so many wishes on that log."

"Really?" she asked, inspecting the ends of her hair.

"Did you put them there?"

"Me? N-no," she say, still not looking at me.

"Then where did they come from? Did . . . other people put the wishes in the river?"

She just kept looking at her hair.

"Meadow Lark, did you tell anyone about that?"

"M-maybe I did," she say.

"But . . . we were supposed to keep that a secret."

Meadow Lark tossed her hair behind her shoulder. "I couldn't help it. How can you keep something like that a secret?"

"Who did you tell?"

She looked down and started counting on her fingers. "About six people, not including Sonya. She was the first."

I blinked. "Well, once Sonya knew, you didn't have to tell anyone else. Kids, grown-ups—now everybody knows."

"But something like that is so fantastic that everyone *should* know about it. I want to see all the wishes on it."

I stuffed my pillow behind me and sat back. "And another thing about the log—it's sticking way out and pointing downriver. I think it got loose because of all the rain."

"Or maybe it's getting ready to float away . . . with all those wishes."

I hopped off my bed and opened my ballerina box, hoping to see my emerald ring in there. Until the day my ring come back to me, I would always open that box and hope to see it.

"You'll find your ring," Meadow Lark say quietly. "I just know it. Let's go one more time before the log floats away and wish for your ring."

I began putting away the stuff that was on my bed. Meadow Lark come over and help me. "You're so sure wishes come true," I say, and she nodded.

There was something strange, different, magical about that log. "Okay," I say. "Let's go one more time."

Chapter 19

When I was sure Mama and Daddy were asleep, I nodded to Meadow Lark. Then I got the flashlight from my room, and Meadow Lark took her backpack, and we slipped out of the house and made our way to the log. Even though the sky was clear and the moon was out full to guide us, it took us a long time because Meadow Lark had to walk slow.

"See?" I say, shining the flashlight on the log. The wishes were still there, like a cluster of butterflies.

"Look at them all!" she say. "I want to read them."

"Me too," I say, "But do you think we should? They're private."

"We won't tell anyone, and we'll put them right back. Aren't you curious?"

I nodded. "Of course. So, go get them."

"I can't—that bank is too steep for me. I'd fall in and drown. You'll have to do it, River."

I studied the bank. It was about two feet down, and then the water was another two feet deep.

"Hold on to the log as you go," she say. "I'll shine the flashlight."

I studied the water in the flashlight's beam. It was rushing and churning against the log, and I could hardly take a breath. "I can't go in that water."

"You have to," Meadow Lark say.

I had an idea. "Shine the light along the log," I told Meadow Lark, and when I saw again how wide and how long it was, I say, "I'll crawl out to the wishes. Just keep pointing the light in front of me, okay?"

"Be careful," she say, and the light jiggled.

I crouched on the riverbank where it met the log, and steadied my breath against the fear creeping up my chest. The bark scratched my palms and snagged my jeans, but I inched along. All I had to do was crawl out a few yards, grab the wishes, and crawl backward.

The water churned against the log and curled under it, and every once in a while sloshed water on my hands and legs.

"It's getting slippery," I called behind me, my voice quivering.

"Then turn back. It's not that important."

I felt paralyzed, but I had to move forward. The

wishes fluttered a yard in front of me now. "No, I want to do it."

"Be careful, then, River. You can do it," Meadow Lark say, aiming the light just ahead of me. The wishes seemed to glow.

Finally, I was close enough and grabbed some of the wishes with my free hand. Then I began crawling backward.

Careful, I told myself, imagining how it would be to fall into the water. I could grab on to the log, but I would lose the wishes.

Another few inches and my right foot felt the mud of the riverbank, and a sob come out of my mouth along with the fear of being that close to the water.

"Take them," I say to Meadow Lark, holding out the wishes to her. Then I slid completely off the log and onto solid ground.

We found a dry spot under some pine trees, and Meadow Lark laid down a towel from her backpack. While I waited for my heart to slow down and my hands to stop shaking, she tucked the flashlight under her chin and opened up the wishes, one by one— carefully, so they wouldn't tear. Quietly we read each wish as Meadow Lark laid them on the ground.

I wish I had a tutor.

I wish we had more money.

I wish Jacob Sievers would notice me.

I wish my dad had more patients because he's a good dentist.

I wish I could pass history.

I wish Daniel liked me.

I wish for a million dollars.

I wish Ariel Zucchero could love me.

I wish my snaggletooth was straight.

I wish for a miracle.

Secrets are holy things. That was one thing I never heard Mama say, but it's what I figured out as I read those wishes. It's how tiny I felt in the presence of the hearts that had written them.

"Here's the last one," she say, and when she laid it down, I gasped.

I wish Theron would come home.

It was what I wished every day. But even more than that—

"Did you write it?" Meadow Lark asked.

"No," I say, shaking my head. But I knew who did, because I recognized that ratty scrawl. It belonged to Daniel Bunch.

I wish Theron would come home, Daniel had written. It felt like he had seen right into my heart, and it felt strange to know we shared the same wish.

"We need to put them back now," she say, and

folded them all up. "Can you do that again?"

Putting them back wasn't as hard as getting them. When I crawled back to the bank, Meadow Lark say, "Let's stay here for a while and see if anyone comes."

"Just for a little while. But if Mama finds out we're gone, we might as well be dead."

We settled in a nest of pine needles at the edge of the forest where we could watch the beach and not be seen. Then Meadow Lark pulled the Cheetos family-size bag out of her backpack and held it out to me.

The night was hot and humid, coming on summer, and mosquitoes were everywhere. I slapped my arm. "We can't stay long," I reminded her.

"Let's wait a little bit. Something might happen," she say.

I looked out to the beach and watched the river rush by. An owl hooted off in the distance, and I shivered. "It's different here at night. It's a little scary. There are bears around here."

"A bear wouldn't come this close to town."

What did Meadow Lark know about bears? I wondered, she being from Arizona.

I chewed and swallowed a few Cheetos, and then asked, "Do you really think Mama let Mr. Tricks out of his cage?"

"I don't think that anymore," she say. "I think his cage wasn't latched and he got himself out. He liked to walk around the room. And then he just flew out on his own."

"That was his other trick."

"And I need to stop naming my birds Mr. Tricks."

"Maybe he just wanted to go home."

"Maybe you're right," she say, and took another handful of Cheetos. Then she asked, "So, have you been to that house lately?"

"Today. While you and Mama were frosting the cake."

"Oh. Well, what happened there?" she asked, skipping over the cake part.

"This time I stayed, like you told me to, and I saw someone."

"Someone was in the house? What did they look like?"

"Well, I could only see feet, and the feet were wearing fluffy blue bedroom shoes—"

"What's that?"

"Slippers. So I was pretty sure it was a woman."

"Maybe next time you'll see who it is. Maybe she's a"—Meadow Lark turned on the flashlight and held it under her chin, and stared at me with those two uneven eyes of hers—"ghost."

That brought a shiver up my back. "Put that down. It's creepy."

But she kept it there, under her chin. "What were you doing under the bed?"

"I was . . . I was holding a ring. And it looked just like my ring."

"The same one you were looking for today?"

I remembered how the ring fit perfectly on my finger under the bed. And I remembered how small my finger looked.

"It was just like that ring. And it fit me . . . Meadow Lark!" I shouted, knocking over the bag of Cheetos. "It was like I was a baby putting on that ring."

"Aha!" she say, and snapped off the flashlight. All around us, darkness filled in where the light used to be.

"Then what happened? What happened to the lady with the bedroom shoes?" she asked, and I could hear the crunch of pine needles as she lay down.

"She left and went downstairs."

"River, maybe she really is a ghost."

I rolled down the top of the Cheetos bag so they wouldn't get soggy. "She wasn't a ghost—she was only in my mind, just like that house is only in my mind."

"Mmmm," she mumbled.

"Meadow Lark, are you falling asleep? We have to watch, or we have to go home."

"I'm awake," she say.

The moon went in and out behind the clouds. An owl hooted again, and crickets chirped over the sound of the river flowing by. Like one smooth pane of glass that night, going to the place it needed to go. I picked up a rock, hurled it, and listened for the plop. Instead I heard a sharp snapping sound in the woods behind us.

"What was that?" I whispered, and twisted around toward the sound, but it was too dark to see much of anything.

"Maybe it was Mr. Tricks," she whispered back.

I grabbed the flashlight and shone it into the woods, but I didn't see anything back there, either. "It must have been a branch falling down."

"A bear," she murmured.

I turned off the flashlight. "No one's coming tonight," I say after a few quiet minutes. "Let's go home." But she didn't answer.

"Meadow Lark?" I say again, but she had fallen asleep.

By now my eyes had adjusted to the dark, and with the moonlight it was easy to pick up small details like gum wrappers on the shore, or pebbles near the water.

My eyes felt gritty and my body felt heavy. I lay down on my side to face the beach. A few more minutes passed. Meadow Lark's breathing sounded steady and even.

Something moved, a dark figure walking along the shore. Meadow Lark and I were far enough into the woods to stay hidden, and I raised my head to get a better look. But all I could see was the thin silhouette of a person. He stopped at the edge of the shore and then walked into the water, the dim reflection off the river blurring his outline.

I nudged Meadow Lark.

"Hmmm?" she mumbled.

"I see someone," I whispered. "It's like a ghost."

"Mmmm," she say, and put her head back down.

I kept watching the person on the beach. He stood in the water for a few seconds, then pulled back his arm and threw something into the river. He stayed there a few seconds more and then come back to shore at an angle from us, disappearing into the woods downriver.

Who was it, and what did he throw into the water? Was it a wish, and would it end up on the log with all the others?

I was so tired and it felt so good to lie down on those pine needles and think through what I'd just seen. In a few minutes I'd nudge Meadow Lark and wake her up and then tell her all about it on our way home.

"River! Meadow Lark!" called a voice in my ear. It was the lady with the blue bedroom shoes. I was shaking, and the bed felt so hard.

"River!" she called again, and then I knew it was Mama. "Girls, get up! What are you doing here?"

I thought I was in my bed, but why was my back all damp? Then I woke up all the way and remembered I was still in the woods.

Now Mama was shaking Meadow Lark awake. "Get up," she say, fear and worry woven into her voice.

Big, sloppy raindrops fell all around us, and my face and hair were soaked. The sky and the river were colored purple gray.

We followed Mama all the way home. Every once in a while, she turned around and say, "You girls are forbidden — do you hear me? *Forbidden* — to go there again." And then she walked even faster, so that Meadow Lark and I had to jog to keep up with her.

"At least you can go home soon," I whispered to Meadow Lark, and we giggled.

"I'm responsible for the both of you. And with Daddy gone to Baltimore this morning . . ." I knew what she was saying—that she didn't want to worry about us and we had to act dependably and make her life easier. Part of me was happy she was mad, because that meant she was as mad at Meadow Lark as she was at me.

She made us take baths and then go to bed. Just before I fell asleep, Meadow Lark say, "River, I've been thinking about those dreams of yours and the lady with the blue slippers."

"Mmmm," I say. My bed felt so clean and soft, and all I wanted to do was go back to sleep.

"Listen to her. I think she's trying to tell you something."

Chapter 20

"River." Mama was calling me again.

I opened my eyes and knew I was in my bedroom. Saturday morning, no school, and I stretched under the covers. Then I woke up a little bit more and remembered last night and early in the morning, and Mama catching us down by the beach.

"River," she called again.

"Coming," I say, and tossed back my covers.

I found Mama sitting up in bed, her knees making a mountain under her chenille bedspread. "River, honey, come sit with me. But close the door—I don't want anyone to hear."

I did as she told me and then slipped under the covers on Daddy's side. When I turned to Mama, I saw she had Theron's trophy on her night table.

So that's where it went, I thought. Maybe Meadow Lark had nothing to do with Theron's trophy.

"Is this about last night?" I asked.

"No," Mama say. "No more about that. I just want to talk to you, River."

She took a sharp breath and then asked, "What do you know about Meadow Lark?"

"Well . . . I know she likes Cheetos and she has scars on her stomach that she doesn't want anyone to see. And she moved here from Arizona."

"But where did she *come* from? Where was she born, what's her family like?"

"I know she lived in lots of other places. And she likes birds."

Mama ran her hand back and forth across a patch of her chenille bedspread. "Yes, that Mr. Tricks," she say. "He's been quiet lately."

"Well, that's because he's gone."

"Gone?"

"You didn't know that?" I say.

"I don't know much that goes on in this house," Mama say, and drop her hand flat on the bedspread. "Obviously."

By that I know she meant she didn't know about us going out last night.

"But you don't like birds . . . ," I say, but I couldn't finish and looked down. "Never mind," I mumbled.

"I don't like birds, and what, River?" Mama asked. She gently cupped my chin in her hand

and urged it upward until my eyes met hers.

"Well, you don't like birds, and Meadow Lark thought that you . . ."

Surprise bloomed in Mama's eyes. "She thought *I* did something to that bird?"

"No—she just wondered."

"Of course I didn't do anything to him. Do you think I did?"

I just knew by the shock on her face that she didn't have anything to do with Mr. Tricks. "No, not anymore."

I was right all along. Of course Mama wouldn't harm Mr. Tricks, and guilt seared my chest knowing I'd let Meadow Lark make me doubt Mama.

"That girl is a puzzle," she say, getting back to Meadow Lark. "Have you ever met her father?"

I shook my head. "No, but he's been sending her those letters since he went into the field. And she say she was going to give you his phone number."

"Well, I didn't get his phone number, and what letters?"

"The ones he's been sending . . . she say she was going to show you."

"I haven't seen any letters," Mama say, scrunching up her eyebrows. "What about her mother—where is she?"

I shrugged. "Meadow Lark say she doesn't have one."

"Well, she did seem to appear out of nowhere."

"No, she appeared out of Arizona."

At that, Mama smiled, and I smiled back. It felt good to know Mama had the same doubts about Meadow Lark that I had. In her way Meadow Lark brought Mama and me closer.

"Mama, we might not know much about Meadow Lark, but I like her a lot. She come here when I needed her."

"For me, too."

"You mean because of Theron?"

Mama just nodded and picked at the bedspread.

"I want to know," I say, "what happened to you that first night Meadow Lark ate supper with us?"

"What do you mean?"

"You know—you got up in the middle of supper and went to bed, and the next morning you started humming again. I thought it had to do with Meadow Lark, like you saw something you've been looking for."

"Well," Mama say, bunching up the bedspread in her hands, "it was strange. What do you think I saw?"

"Promise me you won't laugh," I say, and when she crossed her heart, I say, "Maybe you saw an angel."

Mama didn't laugh. She looked very solemn.

"Promise you won't laugh? I thought I did—but just for a moment. Then I realized it was just my imagination playing tricks with the candlelight."

A little part of me was disappointed to hear that. Every once in a while I wanted to be able to believe, to hope that it was true. But if Mama didn't think so, then there was no reason to wonder.

"But ever since then, you've been a lot happier, and . . ." My eyes burned with tears.

"Honey?"

"It's like you're not sad anymore about Theron. It's like you forgot all about him."

"Forgot about Theron? I could never forget about your brother. He's with me every minute of every day."

That was the first time ever that Mama and I talked about Theron since he left us, and talking about him made it feel like a little bit of him had come back to us.

"Why doesn't anyone here ever talk about him?" I asked.

"River, just because you don't talk about something doesn't mean you're not thinking about it."

"Is that why his trophy is in your room, because you're thinking about Theron?" I asked, looking at it. "I thought Meadow Lark took it."

"Yes, you could say that," she say, touching it. "I

missed your brother, and this made me feel closer to him."

"But you didn't do anything to stop him when he went away. It's like you *wanted* him to leave."

"He needed to leave."

"No, he didn't." My voice come bouncing out, tripping over my tears, and I swiped at my cheeks. "You and Daddy drove him away!" I say. That warm, close feeling with Mama had disappeared.

She patted the fringe in her hand like it was a small animal. "Honey, this talk will get us nowhere. Let's get breakfast started."

"No, I want to talk about Theron."

"We've talked enough about your brother."

"Well, I haven't even started talking about Theron." I loved saying his name and hearing it spoken, even in this conversation, and wanted to say it again and again.

"He chose to go when he took that boy in the car after he was drinking and then drove off the road."

"Do you really think Theron did that?"

"I didn't want to."

"Well, I don't believe he did. It *can't* be true."

Then Mama did something I never saw her do before. She bunched up her bedspread with both hands and pressed it to her eyes, and her forehead and cheeks grew as pink as a watermelon. Mama was crying so quietly. And then my tears fell too, just as quiet, and I snuggled close to her. After a little while like that, she took the bedspread from her face and wrapped her arms around me.

"My heart feels like it was clawed out," Mama say.

"I know—that's how I feel too."

"I don't even care anymore if it's true or not," she say. "I just wish he were home with us."

It had been forever since Mama and I had talked like this, and I didn't want the conversation to end yet. I still had questions.

"Why did you make that cake with Meadow Lark? We make that cake together every summer."

"That was just a cake, River, not a birthday cake. I mean—" Suddenly, Mama swung her legs over the side of the bed. "Let's get up now, River. I have a lot to do today."

But I didn't move. "Whose birthday?" I asked.

Mama had so many secrets. Theron, June at the cemetery, the non-birthday cake we made for nobody . . . "Mama, Daddy say June R. Wadleigh was your best friend, like a sister."

Mama nodded.

"Well, what happened to her? How did she die?"

Mama looked down at her hands. "She was on a bridge, and there was a flood and . . ."

"Daddy tried to save her."

Mama turned to me, looking surprised. "How did you know about that? We—"

"The men were talking about it at church," I say, and the pieces of Mama's and Daddy's secrets were starting to fit together.

"Well, now you know why we don't want you down there, why I got so upset this morning. It was terrible, just terrible." Mama pushed her dark hair off her face. "I don't want anything to happen to you, ever. Do you understand? You don't know what can happen when the water rises."

I nodded. "I understand."

Then, instead of getting up to start the day, Mama sat back against the pillows and fiddled with her fingers. She was planning to say something, so I kept quiet. Finally, she say. "Promise you won't think I'm crazy?"

I crossed my heart.

"Well, that angel I thought I saw . . . for a second or two . . . I thought it was June."

"You thought Meadow Lark was an angel that looked like June?"

Mama turned to me, with what looked like a

question in her eyes. "You promised," she say.

"I don't think you're crazy, Mama. I think you saw . . . what you were looking for."

She nodded and I gave her a hug, and we stayed like that for a little while.

When it was time to get up, she say, "Friends are so precious. You should do everything you can to keep your friendships. Don't be angry or jealous. Just love her."

"I promise." I knew Mama was thinking about June. "So, you're not going to send Meadow Lark home, even though she's a puzzle?"

"Of course not," she say, and touched my cheek. "I like Meadow Lark. And she can stay as long as she wants."

Chapter 21

"**Where are you going now?**" Meadow Lark asked the next day.

"No place special."

Meadow Lark had caught me just as I'd gotten my bike down from the hook in the garage. I wanted to go by myself, without Meadow Lark tagging along, but I hadn't moved fast enough.

"Just tell me where you're going," she say.

"I'll be back in a few hours."

I'd listened to what Mama told me about friendship, and I tried not to let anything come between Meadow Lark and me. But something still bristled inside me and made it hard to tell Meadow Lark everything

I threaded my arms through my backpack and adjusted the straps. It felt heavy loaded with Mama's spade and garden gloves and the watering can.

"What do I tell your mama? She won't like that you left."

"Well, I have to do this, so tell her I'll be back in a few hours. When she finds out where I went, she won't mind." After our talk the day before, I knew Mama would understand.

First I rode to Pike's Nursery and picked out a pot of lilies.

"They're on sale today," Mrs. Pike say. "Buy one, get one. How about it? Your mother likes lilies. You want to make her happy, don't you?"

I was convinced. "More than anything," I say.

She set both pots in a paper shopping bag, which I hung on my handlebars as I rode to the cemetery.

After Mama told me about June, I'd wanted to visit her on my own, without Mama and Daddy. That she was Mama's best friend and that Daddy had tried to save her life made her feel like a cousin. Because Mama loved June so much, I wanted to love her too, and being nice to June would be like being nice to Mama. So I figured that taking flowers to her today would be a good start.

I set my bike against a tree and carried the bag over to June's stone. Then I knelt down and pulled out the watering can, the gloves, and the spade, and began digging out the daffodils that Mama planted the last time she come.

I turned one of the lily pots upside down and eased the flower and the root ball out of the pot, just like I'd seen Mama do a hundred times. Then I put the lily in the hole the daffodil come out of. It made my shoulders ache, so I sat straight up and rolled my head and shoulders. When I looked up, I saw Meadow Lark pushing a big bike up the gravel path.

She waved at me and called, "River!"

"Great," I muttered. I'd told her I wanted to be alone.

Ignoring her for a moment, I bent back down and put the dirt over the lily. Meadow Lark parked her bike and walked over to me. "Your mama thought you'd be here."

That made me feel good. It meant Mama knew what was important to me.

"Then she went for a walk," she say, "so I couldn't ask her which bike to take."

I glanced at the bike she had parked next to mine. "That's Theron's bike! You can't touch that bike — no one can. You have to take it back, Meadow Lark."

"Sorry — I didn't know. It was just the first one I saw."

My heart was bloated with anger at her, and I couldn't keep it in anymore. "You took my room, you took my mama, and now you're taking my brother's bike. Why don't you just move in and take over my whole family?"

"Oh, if I did that," she say, looking puzzled, "would you still be there?"

"Meadow Lark . . . I thought we were friends."

"But aren't we?" she asked.

"Sometimes I'm not sure."

"River," she say, kneeling down beside me, "I'm really sorry. I didn't mean to do any of those things, honest. I'm just not good at being a friend. I've never really had one because we move all the time."

"Wait," I say, "does that mean you'll move away from here, too?"

"I hope not, but we might. My dad's job moves us all over the place."

"Well, I don't want you to leave," I say. I just wanted to be friends with her. I wanted everything to be okay between us.

She turned toward the bike and say, "I'll take it home now."

"You're here now, so you might as well stay," I say. "But take it straight home when we're done, okay?"

She smiled. "Okay, good," she say, and in that

moment I knew we were friends again. Meadow Lark didn't mean to do the things she did—it was just her way.

"Who is this?" she asked, turning to June's headstone.

"She was Mama's best friend, but she died."

"Obviously," she say, and laughed a little.

I laughed too, and then say, "I'm almost done planting the flower, and then I just need to water it."

"I'll get that," she say, and filled the watering can from the faucet poking out of the ground. With me planting and her watering, we took care of June together.

"Where are you going to plant that one?" she asked, pointing to the second lily.

"Nowhere. It was an extra."

"Someone should get it, right?"

"Mama always takes the extras to the hospital," I say, and thought. "Meadow Lark, can you take my backpack home? I have somewhere else to go first."

"Sure, but why are being so mysterious?" she asked.

"I'll tell you when I get home."

"Is Benjamin still here?" I asked at the nurses' desk.

"Last name?"

"You know—that boy with the big cast."

"Dunne, Benjamin . . . yes, he's still here, but he's

waiting to go home, so you'd better hurry." Then he stared very obviously at the lily pot.

"Thanks," I say, and hurry down the hall to Benjamin's room.

Benjamin was sitting up in a chair when I got to his room. His leg, now in a black boot up to his knee, was propped on the edge of the bed, and he was reading a comic book of *Treasure Island*.

"Hello, River," he say.

"How's your leg?" I asked.

"Password?"

"Jim — too easy."

"Amazing. It's almost good as new," Benjamin say, and tapped the boot.

"You heal fast," I say.

"Will you have a seat?" he asked, waving to another chair. "I'm afraid I have nothing to offer you for refreshments, as I've been discharged."

"No, thanks. I just come here to ask you a question."

"You still have that charming way of speaking," he say, and smile. "What's your question?"

"Have you ever tutored anyone before?"

"I have. I'm especially good at science and math and literature, and not as good at history or other languages, except Latin. Do you need a tutor?"

"Not me. Do you remember Daniel, the boy across the hall?"

"The boy who almost died. I scared you then, didn't I? I apologize for that. But actually, he did seem a bit lifeless for a few days."

"So you can tutor Daniel in science and math?"

"Certainly. If he'd like me to."

"Good," I say. "These are for you."

"And if I'd said I wouldn't tutor him?" he asked.

"They would still be for you."

Just then, the feather I'd caught the day before started prickling me through my shorts. I set the lily on his rolling tray and scratched my thigh.

"Thank you," Benjamin say. "As you can see, my room has no flowers, so thank you for these. . . . Is something wrong?"

"No . . . yes," I say, and pulled the feather out of my pocket. "This was poking me."

Benjamin studied the feather in my hand. "If I were you, I would take note of that. Poking generally means your attention is desired."

"It's a feather, Benjamin."

"Ah, but from what . . . or whom? Do you know someone with white feathers?"

"Only Mr. Tricks."

"Then perhaps Mr. Tricks is trying to tell you

something," he say. Then he picked up his comic book and continued reading it.

Was Benjamin right? Was Mr. Tricks trying to tell me something?

If the feather come from across the river, I thought, maybe that's where Mr. Tricks was. But that would mean I'd have to cross the bridge to get there.

Chapter 22

I rode down the old path in back of the baseball field, until it got so overgrown with weeds that I had to get off my bike and walk it. I had never been this way to the river, and by the look of the path, neither had many other people for a long time.

It had started raining hard, and the river looked like a stream of boiling milk, all stirred up with the spray of raindrops. Ahead of me loomed the covered bridge, dark and grim. Just looking at it turned my feet into blocks of ice, and I thought of many reasons not to cross it.

All you have is a feather, I thought. *You're not even sure where it come from. You don't even know that feather come off Mr. Tricks.* And the worst of them all: *That bird is probably already dead.*

No. I had to keep going. I had to look for Mr. Tricks on the other side of the river. If I didn't find him there, then I could stop looking.

I had reached the bridge. It looked like a dark mouth open wide to swallow me, and a sour smell of wet wood and moss and decaying fish surrounded it. My pulse thrummed in my ears as I set my bike down.

I stepped onto the abutment, my legs wobbling and my heart pounding, and looked down the cavernous length of the bridge. The water below me on both sides of the bank roared and churned, making me dizzy. Some of the planks in the bridge's floor were missing, and below them the river roiled and groaned.

Staring into the bridge, I felt that cold water swirling around me, creeping up my legs, and tossing and tumbling me until I didn't know which way was up. I felt so cold — and could not catch a breath.

River, honey, say a voice in my head. *Stay right there.*

I gasped and the sensation faded. I had felt that water closing in around me and heard a voice — a woman's voice — tell me to stay put. Whatever had just happened, maybe it explained why I couldn't go any deeper into the river than my toes.

Shivering with fear, I ran off the bridge to my bike. The wind twisted around me, blowing my hair in every direction, and then a blink of lightning and then another startled the clouds. A fist of thunder cracked the sky and rumbled away, blending with the river's roar and the pounding of my heart.

I would have to let Mr. Tricks go. It made me sad, but I couldn't cross that bridge. I might never cross that bridge.

I grabbed my bike and looked at the path to the baseball field. It had become a lake.

Chapter 23

Dusk was happening somewhere above those thick clouds. There, the sun set under the horizon, the moon rose, and the grit of stars rubbed through the sky until it sparkled. But below those clouds was just a lot of rain.

When I come home from the bridge, instead of going inside, I went straight to the deck and sat and watched raindrops shimmy across the hem of the awning and fall in big, sloppy drops. They crackled the trees and pattered in the grass, and drew the rich earth smells from the ground.

Daddy had come back from Baltimore. As I sat on the deck, I heard the kitchen door open and then his footsteps beside me.

"What are you doing out here, honey?" he asked, dragging a chair next to mine. "You missed supper, and Mama was worried."

"I'm just listening . . . and thinking."

"She also wanted to bake with you."

"Why didn't she ask Meadow Lark?"

"Because she wanted you."

"Daddy, I miss you when you go away. I miss everyone when they go away. Every single person."

Daddy looked out into the rain for a long time, and then he say, "So do I, River."

"Even Theron?"

He nodded just the slightest. "Theron especially right now."

"But you were mad at him."

"I was. Nothing says I can't be mad at him and miss him at the same time."

"But you made him go away."

Daddy was silent for a while and then he say, "He's lucky no one pressed charges against him. That's one thing he's got on his side. So wherever he is, he's not running from the law."

"Do you love Theron?"

Daddy shifted in his chair. The smell of supper come off him, and he say, "I love your brother with everything in me."

Just like Mama. They both loved Theron, and they both missed him.

"Then why didn't you go after him? Why didn't you look for him? How can he know you love him if you don't try to find him?"

Daddy shifted in his chair and say, "Your brother has to make his own choices."

"Well, what would you do if he come back? Would you send him away again?"

When Daddy spoke next, his voice come out a thin ribbon. "If your brother ever chose to come back home, I would run out the front door and meet him in the street. And then I would make him supper and serve it to him on your mother's best china."

"The gold-rim ones?"

He laughed softly. "Yes."

"But what about the crash and the police and . . . Daniel?"

When Daddy talked next, his voice wobbled like that time we skidded across the highway in the rain. "It doesn't matter anymore what kind of trouble your brother got himself into. I'd do anything for him, no matter what."

Theron can come home now, I thought, and smiled. *I just have to find him.*

We sat quietly like that for a minute or so, and then he asked, "Is there something else on your mind?"

I nodded. "I want . . . I need to know where I come from. You and Mama always shushed me when I was little, but I really want to know about my mama."

Daddy leaned forward on his elbows. "Honey, why do you want to know that?"

"Why did my birth mama let me go? Didn't she love me enough to keep me?"

This time he didn't wait to answer, and he say so softly. "She loved you so much, River. Who could *not* love you?"

"Then why did she let me go? How can you let go of someone you love?"

"She let you go because she loved you that much . . ."

Daddy's voice trailed off, and then he took a breath as if he was going to say something more, but instead he just gripped the arms of the chair. I knew that Daddy wasn't going to answer all my questions. Maybe it was too much for him all at once, so I changed the subject . . . for now.

I looked down at my hand and asked, "You know my little emerald ring?" He nodded. "I thought I found it in the river. But I didn't, did I? It was my baby ring."

"Yes, that ring came with you."

"Why didn't anyone ever tell me that?" Mama had so many secrets.

"Mama's always afraid of losing you," he say. "She thought if you knew the ring was from your other life, you wouldn't be happy with us, and you'd want to go back."

"Back to where I come from?"

"*Came* from, honey."

"Came from . . . I'm trying to change it."

Then I understood another thing about Mama. "If I ask Mama about where I come from, it make . . . *makes* her sad because she thinks I don't want to be her daughter."

"Something like that," Daddy say.

I saw in my mind the log with all those wishes and the river flowing by it. All that water pouring past those wishes come from somewhere and went somewhere else. The river flows in only one direction, and you can't make it go the other way.

"Mama doesn't have to worry. I don't want to go back or be anyone else's daughter. I just want to find a part of me that's missing."

I watched another raindrop slide across the awning and plop off, and waited for Daddy to say something to help me find that missing part. Instead he reached for my hand.

"I know a jewelry store in Boston where I can get you a nice chain for your ring," he say. "Then you can wear it around your neck."

I wished I had my ring. I wished I knew where it was.

I looked between the awning and the trees, up at the dark sky, and asked Daddy, "What do you wish for?"

"I had a wish, honey, and you came true."

That made me smile. "But what's your wish right *now*?"

Daddy squeezed my hand. "You know, because it's the same as yours."

Chapter 24

After Daddy and I went inside, Mama gave me supper. She didn't ask me where I'd been and she didn't sniff, but she gave me a hug when I sat at the table. After supper, I told her I wanted to make a cake, but this one with Meadow Lark, and she smiled like she understood.

Meadow Lark measured and I stirred. She filled the pans and I put them in the oven. She took them out, and while we waited for them to cool, we made a plan. It was the kind of plan best friends make without having to say many words.

The next morning, Meadow Lark carried the cake straight to Mr. Sievers's room and put it on his desk. "This is from Ms. Zucchero," she say.

According to her, Mr. Sievers's eyes grew wide when he saw that cake. "For me?" he asked. "Why, thank you."

At the same time, I carried a vase of wildflowers

straight to Ms. Zucchero's room and put them on her desk. "These are from Mr. Sievers," I told her.

"For me?" she asked, drawing her nose to them. "They're lovely. Tell him thank you."

The rest, we'd decided, was up to them.

I felt everyone looking at me in art later that day. Sonya started to say something to me, but I cut her off and turned to Kevin Kale. "Tell your daddy to make an appointment for Mr. Clapton. I have a feeling he'll be calling soon."

That night, as I waited for Meadow Lark to fall asleep first, I lay listening to the rain. It had been raining off and on for so many days that I wondered if we'd all soon float away.

"That was fun today," I say to Meadow Lark. "It felt good to make wishes come true."

"I can't wait to see what happens," she say, her voice soft. "River, I'm glad you're my friend. It's what I always wished for."

That made me smile. "Me too." Then I realized that if I was really Meadow Lark's friend, I should tell her the truth.

"Are you still awake?" I asked.

"Mmm-hmm," she murmur.

"I have to tell you—I found a white feather at the

river the other day. It floated across to me from the other side."

"Mr. Tricks's feather, right?" she asked.

"That's what I thought, so I tried to go across the bridge to look for him . . . but I couldn't. I just couldn't go over that bridge. I wanted to find him and bring him home to you, but I'm sorry I couldn't do it."

"I can . . . go there and . . . look for him. . . ." Her voice faded, and then I heard her even breathing, which told me she was asleep.

I must have fallen asleep for a bit, because the next thing I knew, I heard the swishes and snaps of Meadow Lark getting dressed. When I opened my eyes, she was standing in front of my bureau.

I whispered, "Meadow —" but stopped, because in the dimness I saw her open up my ballerina box and heard her rummage through it. Maybe she thought the feather was in there. Then she opened the door, paused, and stepped into the hall.

I waited for her to go downstairs before I slipped on my sneakers, and then I went outside, following her. The raindrops bounced on the street like pearls, and fog swirled through them. Meadow Lark was way ahead of me by then, even with her slow leg. When she got to the baseball field and turned down the old path, I knew she was going to the covered bridge.

"Meadow Lark!" I called, but she was too far ahead and the rain poured down too loud for her to hear me.

I soon lost sight of her in the darkness and the fog, and the rain roared like a multitude of wings. "Meadow Lark," I called again.

Finally I reached the end of the path, where it began to join the bridge. There was so much water everywhere — under my feet, falling from the sky, and rushing down the river. I'd never seen so much water in all my life, and my heart pounded out of my chest with fear for what could happen.

I squinted to try to see Meadow Lark through the darkness and fog and rain. Her black silhouette appeared at the mouth of the bridge. I could tell by the sound of the river that the water was almost touching it. Then I remembered what the men say that Sunday after church, and about Daddy trying to save June. I couldn't let that happen to my friend.

"Meadow Lark!" I called again, not caring if I woke her up.

Then she stepped onto the bridge, into the place where the riverbank ended and the bridge began, where there was a floor but no walls and nothing to hold on to. At the same time I heard a crash against the side of the bridge, as if something mighty had hit the side.

Meadow Lark stopped. "Come back," I called to her, but she was staring at something in the bridge. I looked and saw a dark form standing against the side about halfway in. By the shape, I recognized it as the same person I'd seen that night on the beach.

"Hello?" I called.

For a moment Meadow Lark turned around to look at me, and then she ran into the bridge.

I followed her, running as quick as spit and yelling, "Don't! Come back!" but it was too late. Just then the river surged and washed across the floor, thrusting a log across the gap in front of me. Little bits of paper clung to its bark, holding fast against the current. That was our log!

Then another surge pounded the bridge. Meadow Lark screamed and slid across the floor to the downstream side. "Meadow Lark!" I yelled, and ran down the bridge to her, more afraid now of losing her to the river than of the river itself.

Just then the rain and fog lifted for a moment, and I could see that other person edging his way from beam to beam toward us. And as he got closer, I recognized him.

"Theron!" I cried as we reached Meadow Lark

at the same time. Another surge washed across the bridge, and I braced myself against a beam.

"Grab on to her arms," Theron yelled over the roar of the water. Then he reached me and pulled me inside the bridge, protecting us from the worst of the flooding.

We clutched her and waited for the water to clear the bridge floor. Then he yelled, "Run!" and we skimmed across the few yards of exposed floor. He lifted Meadow Lark over the log while I stepped over it, and then we scampered to the soggy path— and fell, still holding on to each other, and lay gasping for breath.

"Theron," I say when I could speak again. I could hardly believe who I was seeing. I touched his face and jaw, and let my fingers sink into the dimples under his cheekbones. The rain mixed with tears on my cheeks.

"Theron," I say, the way you say a wish, a prayer.

He stared at me, my brother—not a ghost and not my imagination, but my brother—all height and muscle and flesh of him. I'd been hoping for a miracle all this time, and then it come, and he was right in front of me.

After a few minutes he stood up, then wiped his face with his hand and brushed off his jeans. "You need to take her home and get her warm," he say.

"But . . . what about you?" I asked.

"I can't go home. You know that."

Meadow Lark huddled against me, shivering so hard I could hear her teeth chatter.

"But — I just found you."

"River, go," he say.

I knew I had to get her home, but I didn't want to leave without my brother. "But, Theron, you can come home now," I say.

"No," he say. "But I'll watch until you're safe on the path."

I understood something then, so crystal clear that it almost blinded me, about why people hoped. I knew why Mama hoped to see angels. I knew why Meadow Lark kept hoping for Mr. Tricks, why Daniel hoped for a tutor and our teachers for love, and why Mr. Clapton hoped for straight teeth. Just as I knew why all that time, since the day Theron left us, I hoped for him to come back. Because when you find what you're hoping for, you can call it a miracle.

I started back up the path with Meadow Lark, shivering all the way. Every few steps I took, I turned around, hoping to see Theron following us. For a long time he stayed on the path where I left him, but then come the time I turned around and he was gone.

Chapter 25

I put Meadow Lark to bed in my flannel pajamas and covered her with the down comforter from the top of the closet. She slept so quietly that a few times during the night I almost put a mirror under her nose.

All that night I went over and over what had happened. By morning I knew I had to go back to Daniel's house right after school and talk to him about Theron. I had to hear everything, and then I had to find Theron and bring him home.

This time I brought a bag of Cheetos from lunch. They were for Honor, because she had been so nice to me about my collage. When I gave them to her at the door, she opened her hand to show me different kinds of miniature candies.

"You have to take one, or you don't get past me."

"Only one?" I asked.

She looked at the little candy bars, her eyes moving from one to the other. "Two," she say, and when

I took a Snickers and a Butterfinger, she added, "They're from Halloween."

"Oh, thanks," I say, and slipped them into my pocket. I noticed the house still smelled like old fruit.

Then she whispered, "His tutor's here, but they're just reading."

Benjamin, I thought, and when I stepped into the living room and saw him sitting with Daniel, my pulse calmed down.

"Why, hello," he say.

"Hi." I glanced at his leg and noticed it was still in the boot, and a cane rested on the arm of the sofa.

"Look, Daniel," Benjamin say, "your friend is here."

Daniel wasn't wearing sweats and a rumpled sleeping T-shirt with holes this time. Today he wore his regular clothes—shorts and a T-shirt that looked only half-wrinkled—but he still looked like a curled-up old man. He gave me his usual glare, and then looked back down at his book. "She's not my friend," he muttered.

"Note," Benjamin say, "she was the only person who came to see you in the hospital."

"Note—I'm paying you," Daniel say.

"Correction—you are not. And we are done for today."

"We still have five minutes," Daniel say.

Benjamin reached for his cane and stood up. "My ride will be here early." Then he hoisted his backpack over one shoulder and did his little bow to me and left.

I watched him step out to the front door, and then Daniel glared and say, "You're still here?"

"What happened to Benjamin's leg?"

"He fell off a cliff," Daniel say, and glared at me again, as if Theron had something to do with that, too. That's when I noticed Daniel's wrist.

"Your bandage is gone," I say.

"Genius."

His vocabulary must have expanded, I thought. "Are they graduating you?" I asked.

Daniel put his bony bare feet up on the coffee table. Then he let out a big sigh and crossed his arms. "With summer school."

"But isn't that what Benjamin's for?"

"What's with all the questions?" he asked, and threw his head back against the sofa. "He's moving, so he can only come a few more times."

I shrugged. "Before I forget, call Sonya."

"Sonya?" he asked. "What for?"

"Just call her."

Daniel clapped the book shut. "So, what are you doing here?"

I didn't want Daniel to see my knees shaking, so I sat in the big chair. Then I asked him, "How did you meet my brother?"

He was quiet for a few seconds, and then his big toes started wriggling, and then his fingers. "You don't know?"

I didn't say anything, but let him answer. It might have been my imagination, but Daniel's cheeks had turned pink and blotchy like he was about to cry. Finally he spoke. "You know that program at the community center, the one for kids?"

I nodded. That program was for kids who got held back in school and got into trouble.

"Well, Theron . . . that's where he tutored me."

Then I realized that Daniel wasn't about to cry — he was embarrassed.

"Theron never told me that."

"Well, good," Daniel say. A little meanness had crept back into his voice, and the embarrassment was gone.

"How long did you know him?" I asked.

He shrugged and scratched his nose. "A year, maybe," he say. "What's with all the questions?"

"I want to know about him."

"And you think I want to help *you*?"

I sat up straight in the big chair and planted my feet square on the floor and clutched the arms. "Look,

Daniel Bunch, I know that you want to know just as much as I do. I know that you want him to come back just as much as I do. And I know I was the only person who *came* to see you in the hospital. And except for Benjamin, I'm probably the only person who's come to see you since you got home."

The whole time I say this, Daniel Bunch looked at his toes. His jaw was bulging and his lips were moving like he was trying to keep them still. So I kept on saying what I come to say.

"Everyone has a story about that night, but I don't believe any of them. Pretty soon they'll be making up lies about you. So why don't you tell me the truth."

It felt great to talk to Daniel like that.

Daniel's face flushed again and his chest rose and fell like it would explode. He was working up to something big, and finally he say, "You weren't the only person who visited me in the hospital." He looked at me with eyes rimmed red. "After you tried to slice me up, Theron came."

"Theron? But how . . . ?"

"I was asleep one night, and someone whispered my name. I opened my eyes, and he was standing there. He said, 'I just had to see you're okay.' Everyone knew he disappeared, so it was like seeing a ghost."

If he come to see Daniel, then that meant he was around here at least a week ago. "How did he get in without getting caught?"

"Theron found a way," Daniel say, and wiped his eyes. I couldn't believe it, but I felt sorry for him. "Then . . . he told me something else."

"What?"

Daniel mumbled something that sounded like, "Don't worry. The secret's safe."

"What secret?"

Then Daniel started crying and couldn't catch his breath, like a secret that had been beating him up inside was now punching its way out.

"Daniel, *what are you talking about*?"

Turning fully to me, Daniel blurted, "Theron—wasn't drunk. He—was-n't."

"I *knew* that! I knew it couldn't be true—"

"He wasn't drinking anything, I swear. Not even water. I know it—because I saw him."

I'd been right all along about Theron.

"I was hanging out. He drove up and saw what I was doing and told me to get in the car—he'd take me home. I wanted to go with him, but I said only if I could drive."

"You drove? He let you *drive*?"

"I pushed him to see how bad he wanted me out

of there. There weren't any cars around that night, so he said okay."

"So . . . you . . ." The horror split my chest and my stomach heaved. "You . . . drove the car . . . and you—"

"It was me. *I* drove off the road. *I* made the wreck, not Theron."

"Why didn't you tell anybody? Why did you lie about it all this time? Why did you . . . take it out on me?"

"Theron told me to keep quiet. He said he was responsible, and he would take the blame."

I sat stunned at what Daniel told me while he sobbed all over again. Finally, after he calmed down, he say, "I miss Theron too. And it's all my fault he's gone!"

Chapter 26

By the next day, the downpour of rain had turned to soft showers that played tag with the sunshine, and the lake had turned back into an overgrown path.

I paused in front of the bridge. The log was gone. Someone might have rolled it off the bridge, but knowing that log, it probably pushed itself off and floated away. The water ran several feet below the bridge now, looking close to normal. The only thing that hadn't changed was the pounding of my heart.

I took a deep breath and shook the fear out of my body. Theron could be on the other side of the river, and that bridge wasn't going to stop me this time.

I stepped onto the floor and grabbed a beam, then closed my eyes. I took another step, and another, forcing myself to breathe evenly as I made my way beam by beam to the other side.

Then it happened again.

꙳ꙮ꙳

River, honey, you stay right there.

It was the same voice I'd heard when I come to the bridge for Mr. Tricks, a voice from deep inside me.

Don't go any farther on that bridge, she say, her voice fluttering with fear. *Don't be scared, baby. I'll come get you.*

The smell of tar and wet wood and moss and fish surrounded me, and the icy water washed over my bare feet, numbing them.

Why did you run out like that and worry me so? she say. *Why did you go out here when I tell you to stay put?*

It was too dark to see her. I could only hear her voice, so close to me that I knew every word and how it would sound before it come out. That voice—so like my own.

Mama! I cried.

Then someone with big hands and strong arms scooped me up and carried me. The hands set me down, and I heard Daddy's voice. *Don't move, River. I'll go back to get your mama now.*

The voices and the vision had dissolved by the time I felt solid ground under my feet, telling me I'd reached the other side of the bridge. I opened my eyes and dashed off, my heart pounding, and leaned against a tree to catch my breath. That voice—so familiar, so close to my heart—and Daddy's lingered in my mind.

My legs were still jiggly, but I needed to keep going. I looked around for a path, but all I could see was a narrow strip of dirt and overgrown grass to the left, so I began to follow it.

The foliage around me quickly grew thick. As I walked, the river roar faded, and the twitter of birds and the crackle and thud of branches breaking and falling in the woods surrounded me.

I walked and walked, always making sure I stayed on that path, stepping over poison ivy and thorns and slippery vines, looking down so that low-hanging branches wouldn't poke my eyes.

That's how I saw it—a white feather in a tangle of brush, and then another feather. I picked them off the brush. I took out the feather that was in my pocket and compared it with the two I just found. They were all the same shade of white and all the same texture and pattern. They could have come from Mr. Tricks. His feathers could have blown here, he could have been on this bush, or he could have gotten caught here. Or was still here, hidden. Maybe even dead, I thought, and shuddered, but I had to look. I had to do everything possible to find Mr. Tricks.

I pulled away the bushes, my hands shaking, and picked through the vines until I had searched the whole area. I saw a salamander and some shiny beetles on the ground, but no signs of Mr. Tricks, and I sighed with relief.

Then I put all three feathers in my pocket and continued walking along the path. I climbed over one stone wall covered in moss and bittersweet, and another farther along. And then far in the distance I noticed something tall and wide and dark through breaks in the foliage. A shack, maybe, but as I got closer I saw that it was as big as our garage. Then I walked out of the forest and into a meadow, and I saw that the shack was actually a house. Even closer, it had charcoal-gray shingles and faded white shutters and a porch. Several feet away stood a shed off to the side. Then I heard the smooth rush of the river nearby and realized it was coming from behind the house. I'd walked a long way but had been following the river all that time.

It had started sprinkling again, and I watched the house and listened to the rain drum gentle against the shingles and the roof. Something so familiar about that house sat in the deep core of me. I knew it like I knew the sound of the voice I'd heard on the bridge. It was the house of my mind—except it wasn't only in my mind, because that house existed here in the forest, and it had been waiting for me.

It looked deserted. No one went in or out of it, and no curtain drew aside, so I stepped up to the porch and knocked on the door. No answer. I opened the door and went inside and I let my eyes adjust to the dimness.

I walked to the kitchen, where the smell of onions and oregano and apples surrounded me. There was the same long counter and deep sink that I knew. And the same pantry, though nothing, no tomato cans or chocolate bits, sat on these shelves.

The dining room was empty too—no big table, no desk, and the rug was gone, but it was the same room. Everything about that house was exactly the same as the house in my mind except for one thing— the house in my mind was bigger and taller and wider and deeper than this house.

Then I walked to the staircase, and climbed the stairs, recognizing the fern-patterned wallpaper all the way to the second floor. The bedroom at the top of the stairs was dark. I clicked the light switch, but no lights went on, so I opened the curtains, and dust rolled off them and swirled in the dim light. On the dark wood floor was the outline where the bureau had stood.

I heard the front door open downstairs, and then footsteps on the staircase. Someone was coming up!

There was no bed to hide under anymore in this room, so I slipped into the closet and left it open a crack so I could see out.

The footsteps reached the top of the stairs and stepped inside the room. My pulse drummed in my ears, and a scream started working its way up my throat.

"River?" asked a familiar voice.

Theron.

I burst out of the closet and ran into his arms, hugging him tight. "Theron," I say, crying into his chest. Even though he looked thin, his arms felt as strong as always.

Above me I heard a whirring noise, then a coo, and I looked up to see Mr. Tricks flapping and fluttering, until he perched on the windowsill and tucked his wings against him.

"He learned to fly," I say, laughing. Then I held out my hand to him, and he tilted his head and blinked.

"Mr. Tricks," I whispered up close, stroking his head with my thumb. "Meadow Lark will be so happy to see you."

"I hoped you'd come looking for me," Theron say.

I closed my eyes so I could concentrate on the sound of his voice. "I hoped you'd be in this house," I say, and loosened my hold on him, though this time I would not let him go. He backed against the wall and slipped his hands in his pockets.

"How long have you been here?" I asked.

"A few weeks," he say. Then he grinned his beautiful grin, the one I hadn't seen in more than three months and I wondered if I'd ever see again. "I just couldn't stay away. I wanted to come back home. I just didn't know how to."

"I do, Theron. Everything's okay now. You don't have to worry about a thing."

Theron looked out the window and then say, "Let's go outside."

We left the house, and he led me to the shed. Mr. Tricks followed us all the way.

Inside was a little table and a narrow bed. I looked around. "This is where you sleep? What do you eat?"

"Mostly fish," he say, "and berries." Then he looked steady at me and asked, "Have you ever been here before?"

I nodded. "Sort of," I say. "Sometimes I have dreams about the house. I started going to it in my mind after you leave us. That's when I start talking different too. It makes Mama sad, or mad—sometimes I can't tell which."

"Well, it's because you sound like . . . ," Theron say, but he didn't finish.

"Like what?" I asked, but he just shook his head, so I finished for him, because I knew the answer. "Like Mama's friend—June."

He looked at me for a few seconds and then nodded.

"She was my first mama, wasn't she?"

The time that passed while I waited for him to say yes or no moved thick and slow, but finally he say, "June was your mother. Surprised?"

At one time I thought that knowing who my mama was would make me faint or dance or throw up. But it didn't, and I shook my head. "No. I think I've wondered all along, but I didn't see it until today."

There was more I wanted Theron to tell me. "Do you know if . . . did she wear fuzzy blue bedroom shoes—slippers?"

He shrugged. "She could have. Why?"

"Well, once when I was dreaming about this house, I was under the bed and saw blue slippers walk around the room. And the person wearing them talk to me, and she sound like the way I'm talking now. Then when I crossed the bridge today, I had a memory, and the same person was talking again. Daddy was there too. He was rescuing me . . . and rescuing her."

"Why was Daddy rescuing you?" Theron asked.

"Because," I say, thinking, "the bridge was flooded

with water and June come to save me so I wouldn't drown."

Then Theron asked, "Where were you running from?" His face looked like someone ready to catch a person falling out of a window.

The one word that would answer all my questions come to me as quick as spit. "Here. I come from here. I lived in that house?"

He nodded. "They're not dreams. It all happened to you," Theron say, and looked at the floor. "Someone should have told you by now."

"So . . . why didn't they? Why did Mama and Daddy lie to me all this time?" I looked up at Theron and say, "Why did *you* lie to me?"

"I wanted to tell you, but Mama and Daddy didn't want you to know. They just wanted you to forget all about the bridge and the flood and almost drowning. They didn't want you to worry about anything. So I had to promise not to tell."

I knew it would take me a while to understand that, but at least now I knew. "I always felt like a song in the wrong key," I say.

I looked out the window to my house. Everything I knew about that house come back to me. The smells in the pantry, the pattern in the carpet in the dining room, and that voice—my first mama's voice—as close as my own heartbeat. There was something else I needed to know.

"Theron, what was June's middle name? What did the *R* stand for?"

"What do you think?" he asked me.

"Rose—just like mine."

I felt something I'd been holding in with all my strength break and flow, like water finding its path. My tears made my eyes ache, and then Theron hugged me, and his shirt smelled like his bedroom at home—pine and his own skin smell. "It's a lot to understand all at once," he say in my ear.

"I missed you so much, Theron." I sniffled and turned my head away so I wouldn't get his shirt gooey.

"I missed you, too."

"Is that why you come back?"

"Yup," he say softly.

"Now you can come home," I say, hugging him tighter.

His arms stiffened. "No, I can't."

"Theron, it's true," I say, pushing away from him. "Daniel Bunch told me everything."

His eyes narrowed. "What do you mean?"

"That it was him driving the car that night, not you. And he swore you weren't drunk. So everything's okay now. You can come home."

Theron stood up and walked to the doorway. "Daniel shouldn't have said anything."

I knew what else Theron was thinking—that Mama and Daddy wouldn't want him there, so before he could say anything about that, I told him, "Mama and Daddy will have a party for you, Theron. Everyone misses you so much," and I took his hand. "Believe me, they know what they lost when you left."

Theron stuffed his few belongings into his backpack. "This might sound crazy, but I've seen that girl before—the one on the bridge."

"Meadow Lark? You mean around town?"

He shook his head. "About three weeks ago, I was up in Conway. I thought someone on the street recognized me, so I dodged into a pet store. There was this girl with orange hair looking at parakeets. But not just looking—she was talking to them."

"Meadow Lark? How did she get up to Conway?"

"She was the same girl, I swear. And after that I couldn't get her out of my head because she reminded me so much of you. That's when I knew I had to stop hiding and come home."

We had left the house I knew so well, but now I could go back to it without dreaming. Theron held

Mr. Tricks under one arm and me under his other, sheltering us from the rain. I realized that if I had tried to write a wish for that moment, I would have failed, because walking home with Theron was so much more wonderful than I could have imagined. My heart knew what it hoped for, and in looking for my brother, I had found the missing parts of myself.

"Where did you find Mr. Tricks?" I asked.

"He showed up one night and made himself at home," Theron say.

I reached over and petted Mr. Tricks's head.

"Oh, he had this in his beak." Theron reached into his pocket, and then he pressed something into my palm. It was my little emerald ring.

Chapter 27

On the last day of school, flowers of many colors spilled over Ms. Zucchero's desk, and each one of them had come from Mr. Sievers.

"I know someone who got a lot of cake today," Sonya say at the art table. She looked over to me, bouncing her ponytail. "River, is your family going on vacation?"

I was still getting used to Sonya talking to me like a normal person, so I answered her quietly. "Just to Utica for a week."

"Maybe we can do something together?" she asked shyly.

"We can't go anywhere," Kevin say. "All of a sudden my dad's got too many patients." He looked at me. "It all started with Mr. Clapton. Dad's letting him pay in eggs."

I smiled at all the wishes that had come true.

There was more to smile about when Ms. Zucchero

asked me to stay after class. "River, I'd like you to think about joining the art class I'm teaching this summer. It's for students who show special creativity, and it will be fun. Would you like that?"

Special creativity, me? I thought. "Yes," I say, feeling so much happiness.

She wrote the information on a piece of paper. "Give this to your parents. They can talk to me about it anytime."

"This was fun," Meadow Lark say as she put the last of her clothes in her duffel bag. Her daddy was back, she say, and she was going home.

Meadow Lark seemed to have forgotten about the night she almost drowned in the river. I wanted her to think it was all a dream, so I never mentioned it to her.

I was sitting crisscross on my bed. Theron told me I was walking crooked from sitting W, so I was trying to change how I sat. "It was fun," I say, pushing down on my knees. "We have the whole summer to do it again," I say.

She sank onto her bed, and bent down to feed carrots to Mr. Tricks on the floor. "Well . . . not really," she say.

"What do you mean?"

"I got a letter from my dad last week, and we're moving again."

"No," I say. "You can't move, Meadow Lark. We're best friends."

"We can still be best friends far away. And maybe I can come back to visit."

"I hope you can. Let's make a wish!" I say. "But, where are you . . . ?"

"South Carolina. My dad found a teaching job there."

A burst of sunlight grew and then faded in the room as clouds cleared from the sky. The rain had stopped a week ago and everything was drying out. The river had sunk to its normal height, and Daddy say the Quincely town council was talking about rebuilding the covered bridge.

Meadow Lark zipped up her backpack and slung it over her shoulder.

"I'll walk with you."

"You don't have to, you know."

"I want to. Mama say it's hospitable."

"Your mama and her rules," Meadow Lark say, and tossed her pumpkin-colored hair behind her shoulders.

I smiled about Mama and her rules. It meant we were cared-about girls.

"Okay," she say, "but just to the library. I want to look up South Carolina and learn about my next home."

I looked out the window just as Mama was backing the car out of the driveway. Daddy in the passenger seat was clutching the dashboard. Just before they drove off, she looked up at me and waved.

When Meadow Lark and I went outside, Theron come from the garage on his Giant, with his backpack hitched over his shoulders. "See ya," he say as he passed.

"Where's he going?" Meadow Lark asked.

"Tutoring . . . his old student."

Meadow Lark's eyes got huge. "Daniel?"

I nodded, and then remembered something. "Wait here. I'll be right back," I say, and ran back up to our room and took the collage out of my closet. It had been there since the day I'd come home and found Mama and Meadow Lark making the cake together. All that time, the collage was supposed to be for Mama, but now Mama didn't need it.

Meadow Lark and I say good-bye in front of the library. "For now," she say, "because I'll come back."

"Okay," I say, hardly able to believe she was really going away. "You're my best friend."

She nodded and hitched her hair behind her ear. "And you'll always be mine."

We hugged, and after she went inside, I carried the collage down the path to the river. I kicked off my sandals and walked out to my ankles. And then I walked out farther, until the river reached my calves, where the current ran free.

I looked at the collage one more time, touching each thing glued to it—the glass pieces brushed soft, the place on the porcelain doll head where the nose once was, the piece of wood that looked like a hand, the *R* typewriter key, the watch face, the black bear's tooth, the peach-colored leaf that was still soft, the stone that looked like a face, the gold beads, which I now believed were real gold.

Then, one by one, I picked off each thing I'd found and tossed it as far as I could into the river, and watched the ripples slide along the surface.

At one time I'd needed those things that the river gave me, but they weren't mine to keep. Theron was back, Mama and Daddy were happy, I had a best friend, I'd found my other mama, and the song in me was starting to sound just right. They were all I needed and all I wanted.

The last thing left on the collage was the bald plastic baby with arms and legs and head that moved. I picked it gently off the poster board. Then I found an old shingle near the forest and gently laid the baby on it.

Setting it on the surface of the river, I made a wish that the next person who found that baby doll would treasure it as much as I had. Then I say, "Good-bye," and let it go, and watched until it disappeared into the ripples and sparkles.

I wished I'd had Mama's faith from the beginning, the faith that believes even when there's no reason to. Angels are everywhere, I discovered. You just have to look for them.

After I returned all those gifts to the river, I remembered my three lucky feathers. I didn't need lucky feathers anymore. But when I reached into my pocket for them, my fingers touched something stiff, like paper.

I pulled it out. And smiled at what I saw—a folded-up napkin with a little red heart.

Acknowledgments

This book began with a few words and a voice. And then a girl named River appeared who wanted me to tell her story. So I listened to her and wrote what I heard.

No book is ever created by one person alone. As I was writing *Found Things*, many other people stepped in to provide their support, interest, and expertise. And together we told and retold River's story until it was just right. Here, I want to thank those people for making a few words and a voice become a story, and a long-held dream become a book:

My (rockstar) agent, Josh Adams, for his encouragement and support, and a little strip of yellow paper.

My wonderful editor, Namrata Tripathi, who, with her wisdom, insight, and enthusiasm from the very beginning, gently coaxed this story into full bloom.

Steve Copley, for providing his linguistics expertise in determining where River might have come from.

The Nevada SCBWI Mentor Program, and Ellen Hopkins and Suzanne Morgan Williams, for making it possible for me to participate in the 2010-11 session, and for exemplifying the spirit of giving.

The SCBWI Sue Alexander Award committee for recognizing *Found Things*, and for its continuing support of writers of children's literature.

My fairy godmentor, Emma Dryden, for her love and respect for story, and for teaching me to give each story the time and space it needs to become what it was meant to be. And Emma Ledbetter at Atheneum for her careful shepherding.

My tough and tender critique group, the Turbo Monkeys: Amy Cook, Craig Lew, Ellen Jellison, Hazel Mitchell, Julie Dillard, Kristen Held, and Sarah McGuire. Marcy Weydemuller for her thoughts.

Celeste Putnam, for making me laugh and drink coffee and write on Saturday mornings.

Dene Barnett—Lucy to my Ethel—who never stopped believing.

My grandparents, who gave me a magical childhood in the magical town on which Quincely was based.

My children, Julia, Emily, and Andrew, who opened my eyes to love. And my husband, Leon, for his never-ever-ever-ending support. And to God, who makes all things possible, all things new.